Up The Creek

Memories of Growing up in Rural Texas

C.L. Yarbrough

Big Possum
PUBLICATIONS

For information on this, and other publications please visit:
www.possumpublications.com

ISBN:
978-0-9903449-0-2

For Linda

Table of Contents

Up The Creek

Introduction

In 1977 my father announced to the family that he had just purchased our local newspaper, the Evant News and Four County Sentinel. While I'm certain there had been long and serious discussions between he and my mother, the announcement was, if you'll pardon the pun, news to my sister and myself.

The paper was barely a year old at that time, having been started by W. Leon Smith and his father, a pair famous for building newspapers where none existed, then moving on. I think they did it for entertainment more than anything else; the last time I heard from Leon he was running a paper in Crawford that specialized in irritating George W. Bush. Even in the age before the internet, small town papers were hard work for not much gain. I'm pretty sure the only profit Daddy ever saw from the paper is when he sold it.

None of us knew anything at all about newspapers, or publishing, though Mother was the high school English teacher, and Daddy had once attempted to write a book. This was, he explained, going to be a family business, meaning, as we understood it he was going to take advantage of all the free labor he could. As the holder of the only actual paying job in the family, Mother was exempted from the day to day grind. Big Sister had social obligations and an athletic career that was, I think much more important to Daddy than any work she might be willing to contribute. She volunteered to be a roving reporter about town, collecting recipes and fashion tips from the local ladies until she ran out of houses that she really wanted to see the inside of. Then she went back to basketball and cheerleading. Little Sister wasn't here yet, though unbeknown to most of us, she was on her way.

Which left me.

I couldn't run out of sight if you gave me all day, so my athletic obligations didn't extend past sixth period P.E. and B team benchwarming. This gave me plenty of free time to take pictures. I had taken apart my grandma's Brownie when I was six, and was generally acknowledged to be the most mechanically inclined of the family. Since developing photos appeared to involve complicated machinery, and possibly toxic chemicals, I was unanimously volunteered. Also, as I mentioned, there was no one else.

Along with an odd assortment of antiquated newspaper equipment, including an addressing system that I'm certain began life as a Victorian sewing machine and had to be started by jerking on the leather pulley belt while plugging it in, (making sure to get your fingers out of the way before it built up a head of steam), the office was equipped with an ancient reflex camera and a darkroom. The newspaper office itself was in the old First National Bank building, which was, most likely the oldest building in town. The bank was now across the square, in what was unquestionably the newest building in town. The office was the endcap of a business block, each sharing a wall or two with its neighbor, mud-dauber fashion, and like most buildings of this age and style, it was long narrow and tall. The front office, behind the plate glass windows belonged to Jerry Head's Insurance Company. He also owned the building, and was very glad someone wanted to rent the rest. We had a small door at the back of the building, and most of the cavernous interior. The old bank vault, minus the door, was actually a brick and concrete room constructed inside the building. That's where we kept the addressing machine, in case it exploded, or tried to escape.

My darkroom occupied a large walled off space immediately beside the vault. There was a man-sized hole in the pressed tin ceiling where someone had once tried to break into the bank by digging through the roof over a holiday weekend, not realizing that once the hole was dug, they had a thirty foot drop to the top of the vault, and another concrete roof to dig up. I don't recall what happened to their enterprise, I think they eventually gave up and went home.

For photography equipment I had a fairly modern Patterson tank system to develop negatives, three chipped porcelain pans, a red light bulb and an ancient enlarger that was nearly too tall to fit in the room. It was braced with two by fours and guy wired to the four corners of the room. The head was three feet around and enclosed a two hundred watt bulb. To adjust picture size there was a two-handed wheel that would, with some effort raise and lower the head. If I needed to raise it higher than I could reach, there was a small stepladder with uneven feet. Under the focusing bellows was a homemade lens puttied into a hole someone had whittled out of a piece of lumber and wedged into place. A kitchen table was shoved under the assembly where a sizing tray with one broken wing lay. In four years I never managed to produce a single photo where all the edges were square. An ancient mechanical timer that made a menacing ticking sound in the dark, when it worked, was hung on a nail beside the enlarger and plugged into an extension cord snaked around the door. Generous application of duct tape made sure the room was completely light and air tight. On the opposite wall was a shelf with a single book: "Photography Made Easy". It had been written sometime in the 1940's, so it probably matched the equipment fairly well.

In order to heat the developing chemicals to the required temperature in the winter months, I had to pour them into one of the porcelain pans and balance it over a small gas space heater. A turkey basting thermometer told me when I had reached the proper temperature. The chemicals were probably highly flammable. I tried not to think too much about it. In the summer, I just went on the assumption they were as warm as I was.

It should come as no surprise that very few photos taken in that time survive to this day.

My other duties involved operating the headline machine, which required small doses of the same chemicals, loading tape in the Fridden Just-O-Writers, which made copy come out in neat columns, and generally staying out of Daddy's way. He was a perfectionist in his writing and everything had to be proofed, again and again. A misspelled word that made it into print would keep him upset all week.

Computer newspaper systems did exist at this time, most notably the Compugraphic machines that we'd see when we visited larger papers but they were rare and extremely expensive. Leasing one cost thousands of dollars and I don't think anyone actually could afford to own one. What this meant to us was that articles could not be proofed until they were actually typed and printed. Corrections meant re-typing that word, and hot waxing it over the original after carefully cutting it out with scissors, or a razor knife. Since our ancient Just-O-Writers accomplished even columns by adjusting the spacing between words, a correction might require retyping an entire line, or paragraph.

Everything went on the layout pages with hot wax. The articles were glued on first, and corrections were glued to the articles. Inevitably, everything in the layout room was sticky, and everything was stuck to everything else. It was not uncommon in those days to see random words pasted sideways when reading small town papers (another thing Daddy made sure WE never had). Our layout room had once been the bank lobby, and was still covered with a threadbare carpet which soon became littered with thousands of words and groups of words all liberally waxed to the floor. If you dropped a word correction before you could carefully position it with the tip of an exacto knife, you simply went and printed another. Watching it flutter to the ground and attempting to find it again was a fools game, that didn't play well at three a.m. One night, after repeated attempts to get everything perfect were still not good enough for Daddy, I got mad and drove home, leaving him to storm around by himself. Mother heard me pull up and met me at the door. I doubt he had called to complain, but she knew what had happened. She explained to me in no uncertain terms that one of us had to go back and help him, and she was pretty sure it wasn't going to be her. I turned around and drove back into town. He acted like I hadn't left, even though I had been gone for half an hour.

Hard hitting journalism doesn't come through the door of small town papers very often. Shortly after we started a second paper in a neighboring town Daddy found himself in the middle of a story that would lead to federal probes and threats of prison time for the mayor and several members of the city council. Daddy was proud of the fact that even though he was largely responsible for the problems they were facing, the mayor was always willing to talk to him because he knew Daddy wouldn't try to twist his words or take a statement out of context. Others in that town were not so generous, and Daddy had magnetic signs made up for our old blue pickup to make sure some innocent passer-through didn't get shot by mistake. Since I was generally the one driving that old blue pickup, I wasn't so keen on the noble concept, and wasted no time in hiding those signs behind the seat whenever I could.

Daddy has always had a flair for the humorous. When we were small he would sometimes turn adventures he had been on into hand illustrated comic books for us to read. With an entire newspaper audience to work with, he really couldn't help himself. An unpopular coach was playing in a tournament against his wife, who coached in another town. The headline read, "Maxwell Beats Wife". A local rancher was robbed, and a politician was accusing another of fiscal irresponsibility. The headlines for these two stories ran suspiciously close together. (He actually got a thank you letter from the accusing congressman for that one) A close friend and hunting partner was getting married. Daddy proudly put their photo on the front page. Beside it was a story headlined "Coon Hide Sales Down". He once called the Governor a heathen. Shortly thereafter the Governor cancelled a planned appearance in town. Daddy was impressed with the idea that the Governor might actually be reading his paper.

The stories that would become Up the Creek, usually illustrated with pen and ink drawings he made himself began appearing in the paper in the very first issue, though I don't think he started out to make the first one funny. A local character named Big Dan, and his wife were robbed by two men posing as representatives from the REA. Now Big Dan was locally famous for driving around in a T model Ford he had purchased new from the factory. He wasn't a collector, or a car enthusiast, it was just what he drove. It hadn't quit running yet, so he saw no need to buy another one. Collectors from all over the country had tried for years to buy it from him, some offering large sums of money, and any new car he wanted, but he stuck with what was working for him. It was also well known that Big Dan didn't hold with banks, and the assumption was made by the thieves that he probably held with stuffed mattresses. These two young men showed up with clipboards and explained they were looking for a dangerous electrical short somewhere in the system, and needed to catch it before it just burned someone's house down, or caught a pasture a-fire. They put Dan out back by the fuse box, and his wife out by the barn to watch for smoke, and to keep an eye on the porch light while they would take on the dangerous job of short hunting inside the house. Unfortunately for the thieves, Big Dan didn't hold with money, either. Or if he did, he was a better hider than they were lookers. They managed to make off with some odds and ends of jewelry before Dan got suspicious and came to check on them.

Now Dan wasn't stupid, he was just country. He could see the humor in the story, and told it on himself that way to Daddy. As it turns out, most folks were surprised to hear Dan had electricity. The story was a hit, almost as popular as the school lunch menu and news from Pearl. The next week Daddy wrote his first on-purpose humor piece featuring two other local characters. He called them Part Time and the Reverend and the descriptions were so apt that everyone immediately knew who he was talking about. Daddy eventually began publishing the stories under the title Up the Creek and they became well known, locally.

After he sold the paper, Daddy published, briefly, a little magazine called Vanishing Texas. This publication was all about his first love, Texas and Texas history. Up the Creek was a part of it from the beginning. Unfortunately small magazines are no more profitable than small newspapers. Only six issues were produced. His lasting legacy from the magazine stemmed from a chance encounter at Lemmon's Camp on the Colorado River with a man from Valley Springs looking for something to do. Daddy suggested taking people up and down the river to see the waterfalls, and wildlife. He volunteered to loan the name Vanishing Texas to the endeavor, thinking it could only help magazine sales. At that it failed, but the Vanishing Texas River Cruise still sails from Lake Buchanan to Lemmon's Camp.

Up the Creek still appears occasionally in newspapers around the country, though a new one hasn't been created in many years. This collection contains all but a few of the first, which we managed to lose before we knew what we had.

I hope you enjoy reading them again as much as I have.

Hunter Yarbrough

"come and join our Chicken Band"

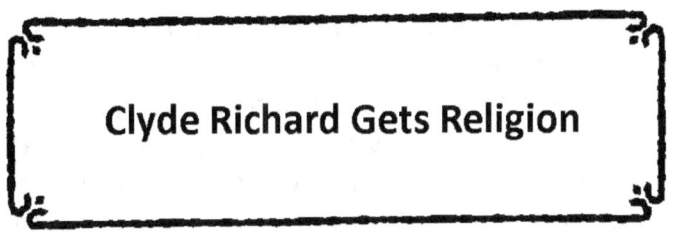

Clyde Richard Gets Religion

My old pal Clyde Richard was the meanest kid in the world. Everybody said so. Adults could sense his presence long before he came in sight. Hardened men would cross the street to avoid him. Women treated his mother like she had just had a death in the family.

My contact with this remarkable boy was through a country Baptist church, where we were both members of the Booster Band.

The job of a Booster Band member, as nearly as I could ever make it out, was to eat cake, drink punch and sing songs for the benefit of the adults, some of whom slept through our performances. Sleeping, however, was a tough proposition with Clyde Richard around.

Our theme song was "Booster, Booster, be a booster, come join our Booster Band," repeated several times in slightly different time. It was custom made for Clyde Richard, who invariably bawled out, "Rooster, Rooster, be a rooster, come join our Chicken Band."

Nothing could prevent his performance. If his parents refused to let him be in the Booster Band, he would sing along anyway, from the audience, which was a whole lot worse. If they left him at home, which they were deathly afraid to do lest he burn the house down, he would walk across the mountain and sing through the window.

We had another song, a holdover from the war that went, "I'm too young to Fly over Germany, March in the infantry, Shoot the artillery, But I'm in the King's army." This song had pantomimes; when we were flying over Germany, we got to flap our arms. Clyde Richard was big on flapping. In fact, he would beat the people on either side of him unmercifully. Our teacher, who was Clyde Richard's aunt, always tried to make sure he didn't get lined up next to one of the smaller girls.

When we were marching in the infantry, we got to march in place. The teacher always tried to put Clyde Richard in a different spot each Sunday for fear that he would stomp a hole through the floor if allowed to work on the same spot continuously.

We also go to shoot the artillery, of course, and this part was Clyde Richard's crowning glory. He would make a tremendous explosion noise, complete with a recoil designed to knock over three or four little girls and a bench or two. Then he would finish it all off with the screams of dying Germans.

The congregation toughed it out for about three months before the Booster Band got the ax.

Clyde Richard's suffering parents got the notion that if they could somehow get him to join the church, and actually become a registered Baptist, he would automatically go to acting more or less like a human being. They kept at him until he finally promised that, on a certain Sunday morning, he would join.

He and I generally slipped off to play until we heard the final hymn being sung, but on the fatal Sunday I got caught making my escape and he ran off into the woods alone.

When the last hymn started, I could see his parents craning their necks trying to locate him. His daddy was turning very red and he was muttering to himself.

It was summertime and the windows were open.

I saw Clyde Richard come drag-footing up to a window that opened between the front row and the choir. Everybody else saw him too, and the singing faltered slightly as everybody nudged their neighbor as if to say, "There he is! What you reckon the little heathen will do this time?"

Then he climbed through the window - about there, the singing almost died out - and shuffled over to the preacher, who wasn't at all certain what he should do with such an irregularity. He soon recovered his composure, however, and had Clyde Richard lined up to receive the customary right hand of Christian fellowship. It didn't happen, though, because Clyde Richard, having fulfilled his promise as he saw it, went back out the window before the first shaker could get to him.

We used to baptize in a long water hole in the Sabannah River. When Clyde Richard's time to be baptized came, he was the only candidate; none of the other sinners were tough enough to be in the same group with him.

While the preacher was reciting the baptismal ceremony, Clyde Richard was trying to catch a fish he saw in the water. So intent was he on that fish that the preacher took him by surprise when he popped a handkerchief over his face and put him under. He kicked one foot clear up out of the water and fought so that he nearly made the preacher fall.

They finally got straightened out, and the preacher was doing his best to restore dignity and somehow keep everybody from hearing the cussing Clyde Richard was doing, which, of course, was what they most wanted to hear. The songleader (Clyde Richard's uncle) jumped up and started in on "Shall We Gather at the River" in as loud a voice as he could manage. He gave it up when Clyde Richard turned and went swimming off down the Sabannah.

His daddy hit the bank at a high lope. I saw him stop in a sumac thicket and cut a club-sized switch.

I can testify that if a boy can be made to change his ways, or can be beaten to death with a sumac trunk, the saga of Clyde Richard would have ended right there. Neither of these things being true, Clyde Richard went on to become a living legend. Sort of like Jesse James.

"I don't know why I ever let you help me"

Weekend Cowboy

I think I'll go into the cow business on my Methodist lease.

Understand, I don't think I could make any money at it: it's self-defense I'm thinking about.

The neighbors, Part Time and the Reverend, are both Ace Reid type cow people, but Part Time stays gone, leaving his wife to do the work, and the Reverend holds an honest job during the week.

Since I don't have any cows, and the Reverend figures sleeping is an illegal pursuit, I've become the official Bee House weekend ranch hand.

I've learned to fear the telephone. Such friendly suggestions as "Come run over to the other place with me" can bring me to the verge of tears.

A trip to "the other place" can mean any one of several things, all of them bad.

On good days, it means only that the Reverend has eaten too much dinner, and wants someone to open the gate for him. On bad days it means somebody is probably going to ambush him and he wants a diversionary target.

He is an exceptionally kind-hearted fellow who never wants to work on anything that weighs less than 500 pounds for fear of hurting them.

On a typical day, the stock he wants to doctor will be nowhere in sight. This means that we first have to stage a cow hunt. The Reverend goes horseback, and I go on foot (it's simple - he never takes more than one horse, though he pulls a trailer around that will carry four). His cows are not exactly wild, it's just that they haven't seen very many people. Understandably, they never want to go just where we want them to, which induces the Reverend to break out his rope.

When this happens, it becomes my job to haze whatever cow he is after out into the open so he can come thundering down on it like John Wayne. They always get into the brush just before he throws his loop.

After three or four of these Don Quixote charges, everything in the pasture is in full stampede. The Reverend rides up to me and says, "We just as well quit runnin' 'em, you're a-crowdin' 'em too hard. You got to work these old cows easy." And off he rides, leaving me to stumble out of the brush whenever I can. If I make it back to the pickup before he gets the horse loaded, I get a ride home.

The Reverend is big on combiotics, black leg serum and ear ticking. (Ear ticking is his favorite. Once when everything else on the place had ear tick dust fogging out it's ears, we tried to ear tick his wife. We got her roped and thrown, but she was such a kicker that we never did get her doctored.) And he has worked out a simple three-in-one system that he really likes.

It goes like this:

1. I catch the cow (or bull).
2. I throw the cow down and hold it.
3. He sticks rusty needles in it and shakes powder in its ears and hollers at me for not holding it still.

He'll come up to where I'm just barely holding my own with one of his pets. Instead of helping either me or the cow, he'll survey the situation, and say something like, "You know that ain't no way to hold a cow."

"This is not a cow," I might reply, "this is a bull."

"Well it ain't much of a bull," he'll say, "He won't be three 'till next month. Don't let him bang 'is head like that. He might hurt hisself."

"I hope he busts his brains out," I'll say. "Are you going to do something, or just stand there? I'm not going to hold him down more than an hour or so."

He'll say, "I don't know why I ever let you help me," and he'll go stomping off to find his medicine, which may be anywhere from 50 yards to three miles away. Sometimes he

14

comes back and says, "Danged if I didn't leave the medicine at home. You just as well let 'im up. We'll have to do this all over again tomorrow. Sure hard on the stock."

Part Time's wife does very well for a woman, but she needs help at times, and the Reverend, chivalrous knight that he is, acts the part of her straw boss.

Part Time's place is close enough that we usually go horseback from the Reverend's homeplace. We usually don't need the horses, but the Reverend likes to ride in like Gene Autry, with his hat tipped back, singing the cattle call.

One time at Part Time's place I got off my horse to shut a gate, and when I started to get on again, the saddle sort of slid down on the horse's side. Everything would have been OK, except that the Reverend (who had saddled the horses in the first place, and doubtless knew my cinch wasn't tight enough) saw what happened.

He first called it to the attention of the women and children (there were only two women and one kid, but he played them like a theater audience). Then he rushed over to me, all helpful, and swung his whole weight from the off-side stirrup, saying he would act as a counter-balance while I tried to get on again.

Now the women giggle when I come up on a horse, and the Reverend has so distorted the incident that it sounds like a major rodeo event when he tells it, which he frequently does.

So, if I'm going to have to work cattle every weekend anyway, and be giggled at and abused, it had just as well be happening at my place, with the Reverend helping me.

I'm not going to buy my cattle from him though. The ear ticks are too bad in his herd.

'He stampeded the cows in three pastures'

The Grapple Kings

I know a couple of fellows who, in the hot summer months, do a little grappling for catfish.

Grappling, for you uninitiated, is the art of catching catfish by hand. Anyone who is good at it – and very few are – can catch a lot of big catfish and have a lot of fun doing it. The only thing is, the State of Texas frowns on this form of fishing.

These anti-grappling laws, I imagine, were proposed and passed by some boys who couldn't quite muster the courage to master the art, or who maybe didn't like to fish anyway. The first thing you do when you want to go on a campaign to reform or abolish something, you know, is to pick something you don't like to do. Then you can really go to town with it, with tears, threats, and noble speeches, because the outcome is not going to matter one way or the other to your personal lifestyle.

Anyway, the fellows I set out to talk about don't pay a whole lot of attention to certain rules and regulations that might have a history connected with such reform measures, and the fish they catch don't' seem to know, being stupid, whether they were lawfully hooked or illegally grabbed.

These individuals in question have caught a lot of fish, and they have told a lot of lies about some they didn't catch, which makes them professionals.

At one time I used to go along with them and poke around under banks and rocks.

They complained that I could never make a grappler because the water level came up too high when I got in, but I have caught a few things, namely one soft-shelled turtle, 2 carp and a bullfrog.

My friends are continually trying to improve their technique.

One time, where they had some legitimate lines set out in the river, they decided that it would be nice to have a small boat to paddle from set to set. But it had to be, they determined, a very small, light boat so that they could carry it around easily.

The only boat that seemed to fit their needs was a child's toy, an inflatable rubber boat.

The grand launching was a brief ceremony, and the maiden voyage was rather short. When the chief grappler stepped from the bank to mid-ship, the stern flew up and hit him in his stern, the bow whacked him in the belly, and he went down with his ship.

Even in the hottest of weather, grappling waters are sometimes quite cold, and my friends believe in comfort when it can be had. Therefore, money being no object, the chief decided he needed a wet suit, an item which neither he, nor anybody we knew had ever actually seen.

He ordered the thing, and eventually it came in the mail. Dumped out in the floor, it looked like a giant, vividly blue dead frog. When the chief got into it, it still looked like a dead frog.

The first time he wore it to the river, he stampeded the cows in three pastures.

It also turned out that the suit held air and made him float. This, he said, was only a minor problem; I could hold him under by placing a foot on him.

I had been wanting to put a foot on him for quite a while, and I was agreeable to the arrangement. I was amazed, though, at how short a time he could hold his breath; I'd always thought he could stay under for three or four minutes at a time, and I did my best to hold him under at least that long. He created quite a problem getting stuck face down in the mud and all.

We used to run one end of a long line through the mouths of fish we'd caught, and tie the other end around somebody's waist. This way we could go on with our searching under banks and rocks while the fish swam along with us.

One day I had about a twenty-pounder tied to me in this fashion, and I had towed him along for an hour or two when we encountered another party of men engaged in the same business we were.

After both sides had first stampeded, then sneaked back to recognize one another, we all went along together for awhile, seven men in all.

I was feeling around, coon fashion, when I felt a good fish. He was lying out in the open between two rocks, and I didn't want to disturb him too much without some help in hemming him up. I backed off and announced that I had a big one located. Everybody gathered around. While we were getting positioned, the chief asked if he was as big as the one we already had.

"Oh," I said, "I think he's quite a bit bigger." When everybody was ready, the chief announced that he'd better make the catch himself, since I was likely to lose him.

I offered an opinion on that, but nobody paid much attention.

The chief made his grab, and came up with the fish.

"Well, lookee here," he said, "don't this beat all? He's just exactly the same size as that other 'un. He's even got the same color eyes. And, would you believe this? He's even got a cord in his mouth already, and he's done tied hisself to the genius here."

My reputation thus established, I retired from grappling.

My friends have long been the immodest grappling kings of their home territory, but they had never, for some reason, been able to catch a really big fish in a certain major river they frequent.

Recently, they broke the hex and found a real whopper under a big rock in this river.

He was tough to get at, and they, with an apprentice criminal, spent the better part of a long day in pursuit of him.

At last, one of them got a firm hold on him and hauled him out of the water.

They laid him out atop his home rock where they could admire him and congratulate one another. While they were giggling and backslapping, the fish decided the joke was over. With a neat little flip, he was back in the river and gone.

His recent captors looked at one another accusingly for a few minutes. Then the chief said, "Well, boys, it don't really matter. I don't believe he would've weighed a bit over 80 pounds anyway."

*'Clyde Richard and I helped Homer pick out
a good club to kill all those varmints with'*

The Huntsman's Club

One time my pal Clyde Richard and I organized a club. We named it The Huntsman's Club. I was president and Clyde Richard was vice president and treasurer, which wasn't much of a job because we didn't have any money.

Our shield was a crossed ax and rifle with a bloody-pointed knife stuck through the cross. This was underlain by an enormous rattlesnake that held a banner in his mouth that read "The Huntsman's Club." Above the ax, rifle, and knife was a hoot owl with his wings spread. He held a coon's tail in one foot and a ringtail's tail in the other.

We held our official meetings under a big rock in the Curry Comb Mountains. We thought it ought to have a name, so we picked one out of the church songbook, and our headquarters became the Sheltering Rock. The only way you could get in if you weren't the first one there was to holler, "Oh, then to the rock let me fly," at which the member already under the rock would holler back, "To the rock that is higher than I."

We were the only members because only two others wanted to join and they couldn't pass our Test of Manhood, which we didn't have to pass since we invented it. Besides, both applicants were girls.

One Sunday, Clyde Richard came up to me and said, "Homer Norton wants to join The Club."

"He ain't brave enough," I said.

"I know it," said Clyde Richard, "but he's got three dollars. I seen it."

"We can start testing him right now," I said.

Homer was ecstatic when he heard the news.

"How much are the dues?" he asked eagerly.

"Three dollars," I said.

23

"Boy," he replied in amazement, "this must be my lucky day. I never had three dollars before in my life, but I got that much now." He handed it over.

"What do we do first?" he wanted to know.

"First," I said, "you have to pass the Test of Manhood."

"What is the test?" he asked uneasily.

We held a little conference, and Clyde Richard thought we ought to make him stab Joe Clark. I didn't think Joe would go for that, and we finally settled on an alternate trial.

"The first test," I announced, "will be a test of your hunting ability. You must go out this afternoon on the Sabannah River, and kill a possum, a coon, a ringtail, and a red fox. Then you must bring these animals to us at the Sheltering Rock."

He blinked at me.

"I ain't got no gun," he said.

"That's the rest of the test," I said. "You have to kill them with a stick."

"I don't know where the Sheltering Rock is," he said.

"That's part of the test, too," I replied. "You have to go back to where we leave you and track us to the Sheltering Rock."

"Is the first test the hardest one?" he asked.

"Oh, no" I said, "it's the easiest one."

"I want my three dollars back."

"Oh, come on now, Homer," I said, "It ain't that hard. We do it all the time, don't we, Clyde Richard?"

"Yeah," lied Clyde Richard, "last Sunday evenin' we killed 14 coons and 3 bobcats with our bare hands. We woulda killed some other stuff, but we wasn't huntin' for nothin' but coons and bobcats."

"I want my three dollars back."

"Well, you see, Homer," I said, "that's part of the test, too, and you're sure failin' it fast. We get to keep the money regardless."

"Yeah," said Clyde Richard, "and if you tell your mother, we'll come to your house at night and drag you off for punishment."

24

Homer never doubted that Clyde Richard would do that, and he gave up his three dollars.

We all went to Clyde Richard's house after church. Clyde Richard and I helped Homer pick out a good club to kill all those varmints with and sent him off to the river. As soon as he was out of sight, we ran off to the Sheltering Rock to plan what we could do with that three dollars. We got so busy with our list of traps and knives and such that we sort of forgot about Homer until all of a sudden we realized that it was about dark and time to go back to church, where Homer's mama and daddy figured to pick him up.

We told Clyde Richard's mama that Homer had got mad at us and walked back to the church house. She didn't seem to have too much trouble believing that and shamed us for being mean to Homer, and we went on to church with nobody but Clyde Richard and me and Homer knowing that things were going to get plenty lively by and by.

Homer's mama never even started looking for him until church services were over, and then things started popping.

We weren't quite ready to tell the whole story, but we did want the search party to start off in the right direction. So when they cornered us, we confessed that Homer had actually been headed off toward the river the last time we saw him, but that, when he didn't come back, we thought he must've gone on to church. It sounded so good to us that we almost got to believing it, but the grownups didn't seem to take it very well.

Homer's mama started in to imagine all the different things that could happen to her darling. First, she had him fall in the river and drown, and they all took on about that for a while. Then she got him snakebit, and old Granny Huff got to telling how he would swell up and moan and suffer until he finally went out of his head just before he died. The old lady made it sound so much like it had already happened that Homer's mama fainted dead away. They laid her out on the front porch of the church house and went back to killing off Homer.

Booger Barnes told about a lost boy just Homer's age that went crazy and ran around in the woods naked and wouldn't have anything to do with people when they finally found him.

Rube Berry thought maybe a hydrophobia skunk would bite Homer. Two or three others had good hydrophobia stories to tell. Then they got off on mad dogs, and it looked like Homer was going to lose plumb out until Jake Hickey had him fall off a high bluff into a big pile of rocks. Homer's mama was coming to just then, and she thought Jake was saying they had just found Homer dead in a pile of rocks. She set in to screaming and nobody could get her quiet long enough to tell her that the search party hadn't even left yet, which made some of them decide that maybe they ought to.

They had a grand time of it. Some of them went horseback and carried deer rifles in their saddle boots. We thought maybe they were carrying guns to shoot Homer with in case they found him in some kind of mortal agony.

Somebody turned a pack of coon hounds loose in hopes that they would trail Homer. But they never had trailed anybody and they didn't rightly seem to know anything about it.

The woods were full of men and dogs and horses. They had the whole river bottom lit up with lanterns 'til it glowed like a Christmas tree. Everybody wanted to be in charge, and there was an awful lot of hollering and cussing going on. The hounds thought all the yelling was meant to encourage them, so they found a coon trail and really showered down on it.

Every now and then a horse would spook at all the lights and racket and would come tearing out of the brush wild-eyed and empty-saddled. It was the grandest spectacle since W. W. Wooten set the woods on fire trying to burn a skunk out of a hole.

Everybody knows that when there is a lost child, and you don't find him for quite awhile, and you've looked everywhere except under rocks and in deep waterholes, that you're not supposed to find him alive. That's when you have the womenfolks clear out and stay somewhere in a bedroom with the lost child's mama.

Along about four in the morning, somebody told the preacher that it was time to get Homer's mama home and that's what busted up the party, because the first thing she found when she got home was Homer, piled up in bed asleep.

He'd been scared to even go into the woods, and had stood around at one end of the river bridge until old man Jensen, who was a Methodist on his way to church in town, came along and gave him a ride home just about the time his mama and daddy left to go to church in the country.

It was such a let-down to everybody, finding Homer safe and sound that way, that it made us all mad as blazes. His mama gave him a first-rate thrashing with a good razor strap, and Clyde Richard and I tore up the paper we'd fixed up saying Homer could be buried at the Sheltering Rock and stomped on it.

'Judging by the way Booger had been catching fish so far, it would take him about a month to catch a mess.'

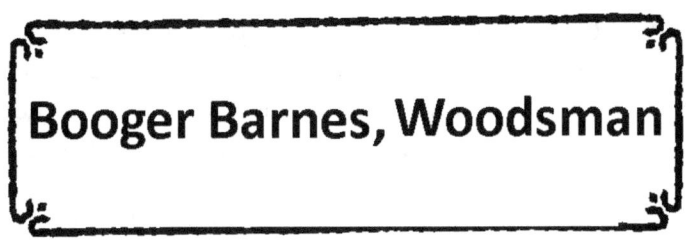

Booger Barnes, Woodsman

Booger Barnes was never what you'd call a first-rate hunter or fisherman, but he never did suspect the fact, and he wasn't the kind of fellow you could educate real easy. There was quite a bit that slipped by Booger, but he was so hard headed and set in his contrariness that he never admitted it even if he saw it go by.

One day he talked Rube Berry into a fishing trip away off down in some canyons on the river. It took them nearly all day long to get there in Booger's '35 Chevrolet, and, naturally, Rube figured they'd stay a day or two. But along about sundown of the third day, when Booger hadn't said a word about going home, Rube hit him up about it.

Booger said he hadn't caught a mess of fish yet, and that he wasn't going home until he did.

Rube said that judging by the way Booger had been catching fish so far, it would take him about a month to catch a mess. Booger sulled up and told Rube that he was welcome to walk home if he was so anxious to go, and Rube did.

Rube didn't have a whole lot to do with Booger for a long time after that, but by and by he sort of softened up about it and could even grin a little while everybody else carried on and laughed real big about the fishing trip, and he and Booger ended up in the same bunch of hunters headed off for a big deer hunt in the mountains.

First thing when they got into camp, Booger made everybody else mad by cooking and eating off to himself while all the others cooked and ate together. He did it because he figured it was cheaper than sharing, and that kind of attitude burned everybody considerably.

Then one evening Booger didn't show up in camp.

Everybody except Rube said they hoped he'd broken his neck or gotten himself eaten by a bear. They even started a pot for a fifth of Jack Daniel's best, and had a fellow picked out to go into town after it when they knew for sure that Booger wasn't coming back.

When Booger hadn't made an appearance by big daylight the next morning, Rube started out to hunt him. Along in the shank of the evening, he heard several shots, and figured it had to be Booger, hoping someone would hear them and answer. Rube fired off a couple of shots to let Booger know to stay put, and worked his way through the brush to where Booger was, thinking all along that this ought to make Booger feel pretty sheepish about the fishing trip.

Booger was plenty glad to see somebody, but, being Booger, he tried not to show it.

They sat down on a flat rock and rested for awhile, then Rube said that since it was just about dark, they might as well camp where they were. Booger jumped up and said, "Oh no. We can make a lot of miles before dark." And he started off in the same wrong direction he'd been headed in before he was found.

Rube was more than a little vexed by that, but he got Booger stopped and told him that he was going in the wrong direction.

Booger narrowed his eyes at Rube, put his hands on his hips, and informed Rube that he'd been hunting all his life, never had been lost, and sure wasn't lost now, but that, if Rube was, he could trail along behind.

That was all Rube could stand, and they stomped off in opposite directions.

Booger drug into camp the next day and never said a word about being lost.

On the way home in a crowded car, Booger fired up one of his evil-smelling, three-for-a-nickel cigars, and the other men insisted that he put it out. He did, but he sulled up after that and made it plain that he was mad.

Rube and Jake Henry had to ride the last four or five miles on home in Booger's car. As soon as they were all in and ready to go, Booger very carefully fired up one of his offensive cigars, blew smoke generously about the inside of the car, and remarked that now he was on his home ground and would do as he pleased. He mostly did from then on, because there was hardly ever anybody around to argue with him.

'She announced that we were about to play tea party'

Brandy and Blue Water

The kind of Brandy this story is about is not the kind designed to be taken internally. This Brandy is my niece. My mean niece.

She was mean natured even as a little baby. Everybody wants to hold a baby, but it couldn't be done with her. From the day she gained control of her arms, she would punch anything that looked like it was about to take hold of her dead in the mouth. Then she'd put the mean-eye on her victim and keep it there. There was no such thing as staring her down. Everybody felt silly trying to out-stare a baby anyway. Especially a girl baby, even though she was bald headed, making it sort of hard to tell what she was (her mother used to paste ribbons on her head to keep people from commenting on her "little football player").

When Brandy decided to be nice to me one day when she was about three years old, I was flattered. She came up to me with a handful of toy dishes and, in her grim, unsmiling manner, announced that we were about to play tea party. She handed me a little cup and saucer, drug up her rocking chair and gazed soberly at me.

I pretended to drink. That wouldn't do.

"No," she said, "really drink."

I did, but I noticed that she didn't. She refilled my cup from her toy teapot and watched until I drank it down again.

After this happened two or three times, I got to wondering exactly what it was I was drinking. I looked in my cup and discovered that whatever it was, it was a pretty shade of blue.

I asked her mother what it was Brandy had me drinking. Her mother looked into my cup. I saw recognition come into her expression. Then she gave me a look of pure sympathy.

33

It dawned on me then that the commodes in the house had the same kind of blue water in them.

"Brandy," her mother scolded, "aren't you ashamed of yourself?"

Brandy smiled sweetly. Clearly, she wasn't

'I heard a faint sound like singing'

Bucking City Hall

Some people are old at 60.

Others never seem to grow old. They refuse to admit that the passage of years should make any real difference in their day-to-day lives.

I know such a man, up on the headwaters of the Bosque in Erath County. He is a great-grandfather to my children, and at 93 is very nearly as active as they are.

He had a little trouble getting to be 93.

When he was along in his 70's he drove his tractor in front of a truck. The tractor was ripped in half, and the old man came down on his head on the pavement.

It happened that he had a headache that day, and had stuffed his hat full of damp rags, hoping the coolness would help. It provided just enough padding to keep him from being killed.

His personal observation of the incident was that the fool driving the truck should have known that he was about to turn, as he had been living there for a good many years and everybody knew it.

He came out of the hospital with a pin in one hip, and in subsequent years aggravated his lameness by having a car fall on him and by falling from the rafters of a barn he was building.

I happened by his place the day before his 84th birthday and found him whamming away on a flat pickup tire with a sledgehammer, while leaning on one crutch. It made him about half sore when I broke the tire down for him.

His crutch comes in handy sometimes. He told me once that his old bull got a little nasty, but straightened up when he was whacked between the eyes with that crutch.

He kept an old pickup for years that hardly anybody else could operate but which he drove with wild abandon.

One day he wanted to go up to his orchard, and told me to ride on the running board to open the gates.

Everything went fine until we got to the orchard gate. It was too late to jump when I realized that the gate was already open, that the old man wasn't going to stop, and that he hadn't allowed for my added thickness in the narrow opening. He raked me off on the gate post as he bounced past it, and was happily picking peaches when I came limping up several minutes later.

He had a wreck in Stephenville a few years ago that bent his old Ford up a little and ruined the other fellow's Pontiac.

The policeman who investigated the wreck asked him if he hadn't seen the other car coming.

"Of course not," he replied, "I was looking where I was going. If he'd been doing the same, he never would've hit me."

I went to his house with my father-in-law once, and we couldn't find the old man anywhere, though his car was in the yard and his pickup had ceased to exist.

We hunted for a half-hour or so, and we were getting plenty worried when I happened to stop close to the well. I heard a faint sound like singing. I listened very carefully and heard a couple of lines of a church hymn, followed by some humming. It was coming up out of the well.

I looked in, and there he was. He'd tied a heavy wooden ladder onto a rope, then had thrown the whole rig into the well shaft, anchored it at the top, and climbed down to work on a leaky pipe. He was 86 at the time.

He couldn't understand why my father-in-law was upset with him, as anybody knew a leaky pipe had to be fixed.

His old Ford gave out recently, and he got his eye on a low-slung hot rod on a lot in Stephenville.

He got to going down 2 or 3 times a week to look at it and dicker with the salesman, who had a pretty good idea of what my father-in-law might do to him if he let the old man buy it.

The salesman did everything to discourage him. Then he started going up on the price. The old man thought he was slightly crazy and a crook, but he kept going back.

My father-in-law finally got him to settle on a nice, safe, little car that has to be encouraged to run fast, but the old man doesn't like it much, and will hardly talk about it. He really wanted that hot rod.

He remembers ox carts, down to the name of the oxen, as well as he recalls yesterday, keeps up with baseball and football through his television, and believes in straight talk (he usually says to me, "It looks like you're a little fatter than last time.").

A while back, they made the streets around the courthouse in Stephenville one way.

The old man refused to accept it. He was a great big kid back in the 90's when they built that courthouse, the streets had never been one way, and the whole thing looked like a communist plot to him. He kept on going downtown the way he always had, which put him south down a northbound street. Some of his friends did the same. After a time the city surrendered, and put the whole thing back like it was.

And that, my friends, is how you fight city hall.

'The dog was hard pressed
to keep from getting run over'

Ghost Lights
and Bad Dogs

There used to be a certain place near my grandfather's farm where strange lights appeared at night. They were, apparently, caused by luminous gasses escaping from the earth, but nobody was inclined to believe that was the case; the consensus was that the lights, which shot up into the air, marked the place where treasure was buried.

With this supposed treasure in mind, three of my uncles set out one night to find the source of the mysterious lights.

They had a bad mastiff dog that had never been known to run from anything, and they took this big dog along in the belief that he would fend off whatever boogers they might encounter. They arrived at the place where the lights seemed to come from without incident. It was a moonlight night and the big rocks that were scattered around over the ground cast eerie shadows.

Knowing that the dog would sense any presence before they could, my uncles were keeping an eye on his activities. He seemed uneasy. He kept his head up and his ears raised. He seemed to be looking for something that he could already hear or smell, and you can bet that all six human eyes present looked everywhere he looked.

They were about ready to stampede anyway when one of those strange lights suddenly shot up from the ground and that bad dog lit a shuck for home.

That was all the encouragement my intrepid uncles needed. The dog was hard pressed there for the first quarter-mile or so to keep from getting run over and stomped to death.

They weren't far from a country road and once they had gained this clear, firm ground, they proceeded to put that part of the country on the Olympic map.

41

This road soon led across a wooden bridge, without virtue of guard rails, that spanned a deep wash. The uncle in the lead made a sudden stop on this bridge and whirled around to see if anything was after them. Number two uncle followed suit, and the uncle in the rear, who had a long crowbar over his shoulder, did the same. Only when he whirled to look back, he wiped the other two off the bridge with his crowbar. He was so excited that he failed to realize what had happened; he only knew that there was some kind of scuffle, and when he looked, his brothers had vanished.

His bad scare turned to pure, unadulterated fear, and the running exhibition he then staged was a classic in mammalian locomotion.

He clattered into the house and gasped out a horrible tale of ghost lights and eaten-up brothers.

My grandfather had a rather firm conviction that nothing, physical or spiritual, could stand up to his old double-barrel muzzle loader. He took it and a lantern, and set out to find his missing boys.

They, meanwhile, had crawled back up onto the road, considerably the worse for wear.

When my grandfather learned what had happened, he offered the opinion that it would probably be in the best interests of society if he shot all three of his boys.

Supposedly, the mysterious lights and whatever causes them is still there. At least, none of my uncles every dug it up.

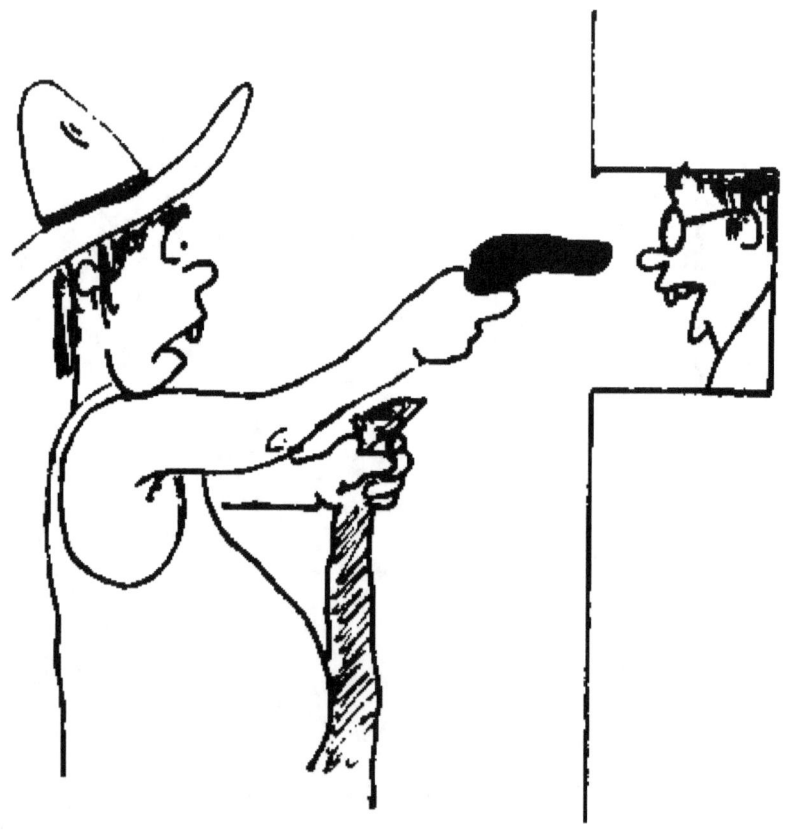

"I'm a bad Texas outlaw"

A Bad Texas Outlaw

Will Evans and Jack Rouse were half-brothers who got brought from Alabama to Hog Town under suspicious circumstances when they were great big old barefoot rusty-kneed boys.

They never could see much sense in going to school or working when there was possums in the woods and catfish in the creeks, so they never did participate too much in prosperity.

A few years after they both got grown, they got to thinking how much fun it would be, since the statute of limitations had run out, to go back to Alabama and see who all they could find that they knew, and how the old place looked and such.

They had enough possum hide money to ride the train to Birmingham, and from there they walked on over to the Georgia line where they had lived when they were boys.

Well, it was a big disappointment to them, because the country had changed so much that they couldn't even find their old farm or anybody that had ever heard tell of them, or that they had ever heard tell of.

They were all down-hearted and ready to head back to Hog Town, but they had a couple of problems; first off, they didn't rightly know which way it was to Hog Town, and secondly, they didn't have a red cent.

They were kind of wandering around without a plan to speak of when they happened onto a big camp meeting. Since they didn't have any pressing engagements, they flopped down on the back row to listen to the preaching for awhile.

There was a whole platform full of preachers and they were playing round-robin with hellfire and damnation, those that were resting Amening in all the right places for the one that

45

was hollering at the sinners. By and by they got the crowd worked up to fine pitch, and that's when a fellow on the front row that everybody had taken for just another sinner jumped up and grabbed his hat and went to passing it down the row like it was an offering plate. It was brimful of folding money before it ever got to Will and Jack, who looked and sent it on by in a hurry, and folks were having to pack it down to keep their dollars from falling off the top of the pile.

Will looked at Jack and made big eyes. Jack made big eyes back at him.

It didn't take them too long to lay out their plan, but it wasn't quite as simple as you might think it was. Jack could read some, but he lost his breath every time he got in front of even a little bitty crowd, and a fellow that can't breathe, can't talk. Will couldn't read a lick, but he wasn't smart enough to know he was even supposed to get nervous. So what they did was, Jack taught Will three or four Bible verses and told him to just throw the Bible that was sure to be on the pulpit open anywhere and recite, and folks would think he was reading it.

Jack got to the next camp meeting ahead of Will, like they had it planned, and got himself a seat on the front row right close to the official hat passer.

Will stayed hid out among the wagons until he judged the regular preachers had the crowd in the right mood, and then he made his grand entrance. He came tearing down the aisle hollering and crying loud enough to be heard two counties away. He had a sermon of sorts already commenced by the time he landed behind the pulpit and shoved the preacher that was already there aside, like, being blinded by tears, he never even saw him.

"Oh, brothers and sisters!" he cried, "I've been a bad Texas outlaw, but now I see the light!" Then he went to lying and told how him and his gang had murdered and robbed all over Texas. He made himself the star of every outlaw tale he'd ever heard of, then he made up some that were even worse. When he throwed the Bible open to Matthew and read the

23rd Psalms without a hitch and bawled like a baby, the crowd was on its feet bawling right along with him.

Then he spread both arms in supplication, rolled his head back in utter misery and sobbed, "Oh, if I only had the money to get back to Texas so I could missionary among the heathen outlaws!"

That's when Jack grabbed his hat and hollered, "Let's send him to Texas, brothers and sisters!"

It worked like a charm.

They forgot all about wanting to go back to Hog Town, and made a regular business out of camp meetings. Jack bought the biggest hat he could find and they preached all over Alabama and half of Georgia, being careful not to work the same set of preachers twice.

But pretty soon it came time for the fall harvest and camp meeting season was over. Jack and Will had been living high on the hog, and it wasn't long before they were as broke as ever, and wanting to go to Hog Town again in the worst possible way.

Will had sort of got to believing that he really was a bad Texas outlaw, and along about the third day that they hadn't had a dry place to sleep or a bite to eat, he told Jack that he believed he'd just have to rob and kill somebody.

Jack wasn't too big on the killing part, but he agreed that if Will had his heart set on robbing, that it was alright with him.

Now mind you, Will didn't have a gun and never had owned one. What he had was a stick he had whittled around on 'til it looked sort of like a gun if you didn't lay it out for inspection.

He stole a towsack out of somebody's barn, and the first place he saw that he thought might have some money in it was a country post office. While Jack hid in the brush, Will went in and pointed his stick at the postmaster and said, "I'm a bad Texas outlaw and you better give me all your money right now."

Will was kind of scary looking even if you saw him every day, and besides that, he took that postmaster by surprise. Will handed him the towsack and he raked everything in his safe into it and handed it back like he was trained to do just that.

Judging from the bulk and weight of his sack, Will thought he must be a rich man. But when him and Jack finally quit running and looked in, they discovered that he had robbed half a towsackful of pennies.

Well, somehow or other, they bought their way out of Alabama with those pennies without getting caught, and they still had plenty of pennies in the sack when they got home to Hog Town. Evidently, though, they didn't invest them very wisely: Charlie Dennis said Will borrowed $10.00 from him in 1904 "until times got better" and never paid him back until 1928, which was the next time he had $10.00 that didn't already belong to somebody else.

'They looked like an army to me'

An Unwilling Teacher

I never really wanted to teach anybody anything. My teachers all agreed that that was good, as, so far as they could tell, I didn't know anything except the way to the gym and the superintendent's office.

It was, therefore, against my will and better judgment that I became a swimming instructor during the summer between my junior and senior years in high school. I worked at a municipal pool, and the city offered free swimming lessons to everybody who bought a season pass.

I was terrified when the list of students totaled sixty-four at the end of the first day, and almost thirty of those were women over forty.

The only women over forty that I knew anything about were my mother, three kissing aunts, and various school teachers, all of whom had whipped me at least once, and two of whom had threatened my life.

I managed to get a little nervous pleasure out of the thing when I discovered that I actually had a certain amount of control over all these people, and that I could set up their classes at whatever time and day suited me.

I liked that.

I began to see command potential in myself, and I spent some time before the mirror polishing my mood expressions, which were designed to intimidate or melt hearts of any age or gender.

When it came right down to it, I was torn between saving the worst for last or facing up to it first thing. I decided, in an uncharacteristic flash of courage, to face the worst first. Then I lay awake all night in wide-eyed terror.

They looked like an army to me that first day. They gathered at the end of the pool in eight or ten giggling groups. I could see them out the dressing room window. After awhile, they began to look all around, and I knew that I had become the subject of all those group conversations.

The pool manager was a chemistry teacher at the local college and before that he had been a Marine Captain. He knew where all my hiding places were. He came up behind me and said, "They're waiting for you."

I said, "Tell them I got throwed in jail last night."

"Thrown in jail," he corrected. "No I'll tell them you're in here hiding and whimpering like a little girl."

He started out. I had learned from experience that he really would tell them what he said he would, and I had to run to beat him outside, which resulted in my bolting headlong out into the midst of all those dilapidated women.

I performed some pretty fair acrobatics to get stopped without falling down, then I straightened up and looked around. They were all looking at me. The silence was thick enough to cut with a knife.

"Well," giggled some smart aleck in the bunch, "our instructor certainly seems eager to get started." They all tittered.

I was standing there in the early stages of rigor mortis with my brain locked up in neutral.

"Shall we get into the water?" inquired some motherly soul, and they all trooped into the shallow end of the pool and left me standing there trying to remember what it was you were supposed to do in the Valley of the Shadow of Death. All I could bring into focus was what my over-forty Sunday school teacher had looked like.

I soon discovered, to my delight, that these ladies were not even slightly interested in my instruction; they were the membership of the local garden club, signed up for a little R & R, and I was more in the role of mascot than teacher.

The little kids were another situation. Each one came equipped with a mama, and the mamas were of three distinct varieties.

The most common mama was a poolside assistant instructor.

The second variety was the perennial debutant who just could not find a place on her country club schedule for a snaggle-toothed first grader. They used me as a baby sitter.

The third mama type was still asleep when junior got to the pool, and wouldn't worry too much about where he might be when and if she did get up.

The poolside mamas could be a big help or a major hindrance, depending on their particular views about junior's welfare.

Every morning for a week I lined one class up against the shallow end wall and requested them, one by one, to duck their heads under water. Most of them did it the first day, and all of them thought it was great fun by the third day. All of them, that is, except one by the unlikely name of Jolly Brown.

Jolly's daddy was a Methodist preacher and his mama was a poolsider.

We went through the same routine every morning. Down the row to Jolly we'd go, bobbing under and squealing. Then Jolly would put the snake-eye on me. He'd turn around, pull himself up on the poolside curbing and look at his mama without saying a word. And she would tell him he didn't have to do it.

It was getting to be a problem. I had to keep them all in one group, because I didn't have a helper, and some of the poolside mamas were beginning to wonder why we never did anything but bob under and giggle. Jolly wasn't showing any inclination of ever leaving that wall.

So one morning I eased up to Jolly and smiled, and told him in a low voice that I was going to bust him in the mouth if he didn't put his head under water.

His eyes got real big and he started to turn to his mama. I had anticipated that move, and I cut him off. Still smiling, I leaned down and whispered to him that if he told his mama I was going to throw him and her both into the deep end.

Jolly understood that kind of talk. When his turn came, he was under water before the little girl before him was up.

His mama ran over to the edge of the pool in amazement.

Jolly came up with an expression of pure delight on his face and bobbed back under again before she could get his attention. She acted like she was afraid all that ducking under was going to turn him into a Baptist.

I guess he never said anything to her about how he came to his underwater decision, because she never said anything and the city didn't fire me. I understand, though, that my methods are not considered good classroom procedure.

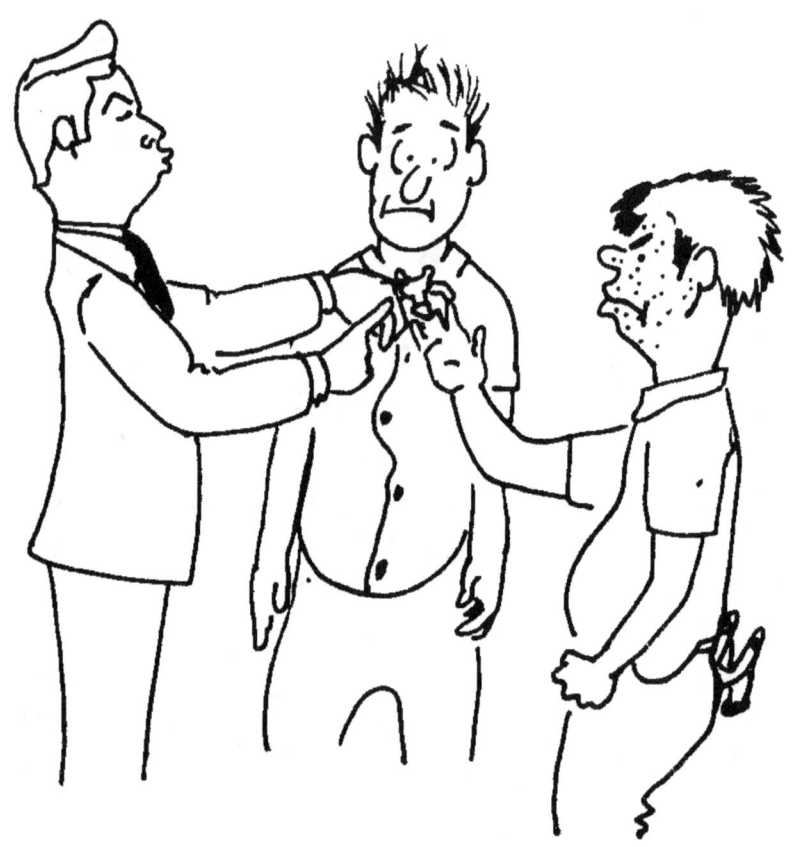

"My father acquired it for me in Calcutta"

Clyde Richard and the Preacher's Boy

Right after my pal Clyde Richard joined the church, we had a summer revival. The evangelist who came to preach the revival had a boy about our age.

This unfortunate boy was a little sissified, and he immediately, on visual inspection, decided that he was more than somewhat smarter than we were.

Neither of these things endeared him to us. But his real undoing came about as a result of a ring he wore. It was a silver saddle ring, complete with high horn and hooded stirrups.

Clyde Richard said to me, "I got to have that ring."

"How we gonna git it?" I asked, never doubting that Clyde Richard would soon acquire that ring, and that I would help him do it.

Clyde Richard was as practical as Hitler.

"Let's kill 'im and take it," he said.

"Naw, we better not do that," I said. "I don't think his daddy would care, but his mama would probably git us in trouble for it."

Clyde Richard eased up to the victim and said, "That sure is a pretty ring."

"Yes, rather," said the sissy. "My father acquired it for me in Calcutta."

Clyde Richard stepped back a couple of steps and motioned for me with his head.

"Where's Calcutta?"

"Somewhere up the other side of Cisco, I think. I don't know exactly where." I said.

He stepped back to the sissy and said, offhand like, "I been to Fort Worth once myself, but they didn't have no rings like that 'um. Could I see it for a minute?"

"I suppose so, if your hands aren't soiled." replied the sissy.

I saw Clyde Richard's nostrils flare, and I knew the preacher's boy was in for a dose of culture shock.

Clyde Richard put the ring on his right hand finger and admired it in the light.

"I am a Royal Ambassador," the sissy said to me. "Are either of you anything?"

"Oh yes," said Clyde Richard, "We are the Curry Comb Mountain Killers."

"Huh," snorted the sissy, contemptuously.

"I think, if you will kindly give back my ring, I shall seek a more intellectual climate."

"I'll give it back to you right now," said Clyde Richard, as he buried that shiny saddle horn in the sissy's nose.

The sissy let out a terribly undignified squall and took off, yelling "Father, Father!" every time he hit the ground.

Pretty soon he had "Father" and the deacons headed our way, which meant it was time for us to go where grown men in their only suits and Sunday shoes wouldn't follow, namely, into the canyon.

Pell-mell down the canyon wall we went, with Clyde Richard's daddy yelling for his only son to stop or else.

We thought we could outwait them, since it was the last day of the revival, and about dark, and the preacher would have to leave, taking the legal owner of the ring along. That time, though, we were out of luck; the injured party and the deacons settled in for a siege on the canyon rim.

Every little bit Clyde Richard's daddy would come to the edge and yell for Clyde Richard, but it didn't do him any good.

I figured we were set for the night, or until my mother sent my brother down to drag us back to the top, but Clyde suddenly announced that we had just as well give it up, and started climbing up the cliff.

This stirred considerable interest among the enemy. They were waiting for us in a little cluster, all smirking except for Clyde Richard's daddy, who demanded that Clyde Richard hand over the ring.

"I can't," said Clyde Richard, sadly. "I lost it down in the canyon."

They searched him and they shook him, but no ring could they find.

His daddy, of course, offered to pay for the ring, but the preacher declined, saying it was just a cheap piece of costume jewelry he'd picked up in Abilene (Clyde Richard almost blew his act at that) and that an apology would be sufficient.

Clyde Richard mumbled that he was sorry.

The next Sunday we went down into the canyon and got the ring, where he'd hidden it.

'Strangers seeing stately ladies chasing armadillos
down in the bar ditches, are a little shocked.'

Crazy Week

Down in Langford's Cove, the folks took to racing armadillos a few years back. The week before the big race, when all the armadillos are caught, is called crazy week.

Crazy week is when otherwise dignified men and women tear through the brush after armadillos, which they gladly ignore or run over during any other week of the year.

Strangers passing through the country, seeing stately ladies in new Lincolns suddenly slam on their brakes and go to chasing armadillos down in the bar ditches, are a little shocked. They make weird reports back home. If they could see what goes on out in the pastures, they would forever after detour around the whole territory.

Grown men, some of them respectable and a few of them reasonably intelligent, fight with one another over escaped 'dillers', each one anxious to pin the blame on somebody else.

They weep bitter tears over unsuccessful hunts, secretly carry good luck charms in their pockets, dig tremendous holes in the ground with sticks and bare hands, run $8,000 vehicles through places they usually wouldn't ride a horse, and celebrate like true heathens when at last they capture an unlucky digger (who is nearly blind, slow as cold molasses, and stupid as a rock).

"Did you see that move I put on 'im?" is a common brag, to which somebody who got left behind will reply sourly, "Yeah, but if I hadn't been over here blockin' his hole, we'd a lost 'im for sure."

Actually, during crazy week, an armadillo who makes it to his hole is still in trouble. He is quite likely to get dug up.

No man wants to go home empty-handed to a doting wife and kids.

The kids say things like, "Johnny's daddy caught three." The wife will look long-suffering, and say tightly, "Well, maybe we can borrow one from someone who knows how to hunt."

Then wife and kids will go off together to some other part of the house.

It's a worse stigma than coming home without a deer.

It causes men to seek out large groups of hunters to run with. That way, they can claim a share of any diller caught, and they can blame uncaught dillers on somebody else in the bunch.

Of course, this system starts family feuds. In a few more years, it'll be like the Yankees and the Rebels. Only they'll probably call it the war of the softshells and the hardshells. Or worse.

"I fell down flat on my belly and grabbed a-holt o' this little bitty ol' tree"

Hog Town Highlights

There is a town close to where I grew up that has never been seriously known by any name other than Hog Town. It's other name, used only on maps, is Desdemona. Some say it was borrowed from Shakespeare, but those who know say that when they brought in the town's first oil well back in 1918, a tongue-tied farmer saw the oil gushing up over the derrick crown and hollered, "Des de money!"

However all that may be, a creek that wanders through one end of town is called Hog Creek.

As long as the town had a school its mascot was a hog.

Theirs is a society that looks upon properness as a form of snobbery, and fanciness as downright sinful. Thus they did not style themselves Javelinas or Razorbacks or any such dignified version of what they really were; they were the Hog Town Hogs, pure and simple. When they yelled root for the team, it really meant something.

The biggest thing that happened in Hog Town since Old Lady Blair beat a crippled Indian in the head with a poker was the Hog Town Cyclone. Everything that a Hog Towner told after that was dated before or after the cyclone, and everything anybody said was bound to remind a Hog Towner of a cyclone story. I asked one of them one time what he was doing when the storm hit.

"Well, " he said, shifting his tobacco to the other side of his mouth, "me and another feller was settin' out a orchard. We was workin' right steady like, and never noticed nothin' was a-happenin' til we looked up and there she come, big as Dallas and makin' a turble racket. There weren't no time to git nowheres, and I 'membered that my daddy alus said to lay down and grab a-holt of sompum if you was caught out in a cyclone, so 'ats what I done. I fell down flat on my belly and grabbed a-holt o' this little bitty ol' tree I'd just got through a-settin' out. The cyclone come right square over me, and it musta blowed 'at tree outen the ground twenty or thirty times 'fore it was over, and I tell you it kept me busy as a monkey on a bernanner farm a-jobbin' it back in the ground every time it blowed out."

Hog Town had a resident scientist, but hardly anybody ever heard of him, you know, because them Yankees was jealous of him and wouldn't let him be known. When the war came along, though, they couldn't keep him secret any longer because the country needed him. It got to be known that he had invented a weapon that would allow our boys to fight not only all day, but all night as well, and thus end the war twice as fast.

When he first announced his invention, some of the people were skeptical; he had invented some other stuff that they didn't think was too great. But they couldn't stay away after he got to talking about how he had contacted the army, and they were sending some experts down to have a look. So one day a group of Hog Town's elite put on their Sunday overalls and went out to see what had been invented. The scientist proudly unveiled a .22 rifle with a two-cell flashlight wired onto the barrel.

Years later he still maintained that some of the people thought it would work, but the 'high faluters' had kept the army from becoming interested.

He was not one to let a little setback get him down, and by and by he put out the word that he had invented a weather vane that a man could read without getting out of bed.

That brought out more investigators than his secret weapon had. Everybody wants to do everything possible in bed.

Since they had come to look at a weather vane, everybody looked up on the roof when they got to the inventor's house. They were surprised to see the vane rod with nothing on it except the rooster. Inside they found the missing parts. The inventor, whom they found in the act of testing his invention, had put an extension on the rod that allowed it to come into his bedroom through a big hole he had knocked in the ceiling for that purpose, and the wind direction arms were fixed onto the bottom end, where, sure enough, he could lie right in bed and see which way the wind was blowing.

"You fool, " said a disgusted farmer, "now you got a big hole right through the roof and through the ceiling and it'll rain on you."

"Yes, " said the inventor, with a great show of patience, "with this invention, I can also tell when the weather is inclement, a feature which no other weather vane before has ever offered."

"Look out! He's right there behind that big rock!"

Johnny Mac Brown, Where Are You?

They don't make the kind of movies they used to. And they don't have the kinds of heroes we worshipped when I was a kid.

Movies of the '40s and early '50s had just two kinds of people, good and bad. And there was never any question as to which characters were bad and which ones were good.

Nobody ever cursed except Rhett Butler in "Gone With the Wind," when he delivered his famous "Frankly, my dear..." line to Scarlett O'Hara. My teenaged brother and sister went around for months saying, "Frankly, my dear." They thought it was quite risqué, and it was, for the times. My mother hadn't seen the movie. She thought they were being nice to one another.

If they filmed "Gone With the Wind" now and didn't tell everybody it was a classic, nobody would go to see it. Unless, of course, Rhett Butler had a lot of filthy lines and Scarlett O'Hara removed several pounds of clothing.

"Gone With the Wind," though, is not the kind of movie I started out to reminisce about; it was an exception.

I'm thinking about the old cowboy stars, who played the same roles in every movie. Roy Rogers could never be anybody else on the screen. Nor could Gene Autry or a host of other lesser-known characters.

Some of these guys had ridiculous names for heroes, if you stop to think about them - which we never did back then.

Consider, for instance, Johnny Mac Brown. What Hollywood writer would give a pistol-toting, rough and tumble cowboy hero a name like that?

One did, and it worked. Johnny Mac was quite a boy.

Or how about Hopalong Cassidy for a macho name?

The Lone Ranger was not the only masked hero of his era, nor was he the only one to have a faithful sidekick.

The Durango Kid, who had a partner whose big act was never being able to draw his pistol, shot his way through many a Saturday afternoon in my life. He played the part of a nice, clean-cut local boy named Steve who would run off and hide when the bad guys showed up. He did it, of course, so he could put on his Durango Kid outfit. After Durango roared into town and killed 85 or 90 people and saved the widow Jones' mortgage, Steve's girlfriend would chide him about hiding while that brave Durango Kid routed evil and brought justice. We kids and Steve kept our little secret, and never did tell that dumb girl.

Zorro was a masked swordsman who had been around before my time, but there was a character styled Son of Zorro that I remember. He played in little skits that always left him in some terrible predicament. These short films were called "continued pieces," and played every Saturday afternoon. If you missed one, there was no way to repair the damage, for Son of Zorro would go on the other adventures.

He had a cute little habit of cutting Zs on peoples' foreheads.

The last time I saw him, his head was about to be crushed by a mill wheel operated by a fellow with a Z on his head.

Lash LaRue hauled around a bull whip that must've been twenty-five feet long. With it, he was much more than a match for any dozen gunslingers.

Lash was an enigma; he was the hero but he always dressed in black from head to toe. Even his whip was black. He was a sad-eyed fellow with a permanent funeral expression.

He had a competitor called Whip Wilson, who wore a big, uncreased white hat, and didn't make as many Saturday afternoon appearances in our town as Lash did.

Everybody knows, though, that none of these others ever managed to equal Roy Rogers or Gene Autry, even though they could shoot 45 or 50 times without reloading and kill two Indians with every shot. (That's another thing: Indians and outlaws, not to mention good guys, don't die as well anymore. Back then, it could take 10 or 15 minutes of staggering and last gasp speeches for a heartshot hombre to cash in. Sometimes in a really big fight, there'd be so many of these guys reeling around the screen that you'd lose sight of the hero. And everybody screamed when shot and every bullet made a ricochet whine.)

I had a friend who hated Roy Rogers. He was the only human I ever knew who did, but he explained it to me this way:

"Six big unshaven lumberjacks will capture Dale Evans and haul her off to a mountain cabin. They don't want any ransom or anything. They do it just to irritate Rogers.

"Rogers, of course, somehow figures out where they've taken her. Does he get anybody to help him, like, for instance, the sheriff? Oh, no. He goes by himself.

"When he gets there, does he run in the door, or even try it? Oh, no. He backs off and dives through a closed window. Then he jumps up and proceeds to beat these six 200 pound lumberjacks almost to death. They get in a few licks, but they can't even knock his hat off.

"Pretty soon, he gets to be too much for them, and they all break and run for it, after one of them slips around behind him and hits him over the head with a 50 pound chair.

"They don't get far before he's up and going again. He's got his woman back and the enemy is whipped and on the run. Is he satisfied? Oh, no. He jumps on old Trigger and catches up with this '40 model Ford they're running down the side of a mountain in. When he does, he promptly dives in the window and starts pounding on the driver's head.

"Now, I ask you, is that the act of a sane man?"

All the rest of us liked Roy Rogers fine.

They never told us until up in the '60s that his real name was Leonard Sly or that he grew up on a hog farm in Iowa.

Gene Autry used to come to the Dublin Rodeo every year, which was near enough to my hometown for it to be exciting.

71

At the end of one of his movies, the girl was on the train about to leave. She was standing out on the back platform of the caboose twirling her little lace-edged parasol, and old fat Gene galloped up on old Champion to say adieu.

"Where you headed, Ma'am?" he asked.

"Texas," she said.

"What part?" he pressed.

"Dublin," she said sweetly.

We felt like we had been singled out from all the world's people for special honor. We walked on air for days. I don't know how kids who actually lived in Dublin survived the thrill of it all.

All those cowboy stars I remember were copies of the original movie cowboys.

These first gunfighting gallants were interesting in that they couldn't talk to you; they could only jerk around and strike mock-heroic poses while their dialogue was flashed onto the bottom of the screen in big, clear print.

I saw one of these once that was supposed to be typical. The hero was a fellow named Red, and he was sitting at a poker table. The dialogue went thus:

"Red sees the cards. The cards see Red. Red sees red."

At this point, Red jumped up and shot everybody in sight with a silent, smoky pistol and rode away.

His flight path brought him to the attention of about 5,000 Indians, who started riding around him in a big circle. Red made a brave stand and had them thinned down to 150 or so before they finally got him killed.

Red died sitting up beside his dead horse. A girl appeared on the scene and commenced piling rocks on Red and the horse until she had them both covered up to her satisfaction. Then she cried awhile and the Indians came up and cried awhile, and the show was over.

A friend of mine who was around when these old movies were the latest in film technology, says it could get pretty interesting.

Only about half the people could read at that time, he says, and these readers would be reading aloud to their non-reading friends and relatives as the movie progressed. With everybody going along at their own pace, in all different pitches, it created quite a buzz.

Some of the readers were a little slow at the task and tended to ad lib when they got behind. This would generally get an argument started with somebody who was listening in but wasn't supposed to be, and there would sometimes be as many as two or three fist fights going on besides the carnage on the screen.

This was all a pretty new thing, and some folks had a little trouble distinguishing fact from film. One time in Eastland, my friend says the hero was riding along looking for this outlaw he'd been chasing. The outlaw was hiding behind a rock with his rifle leveled on the hero and it sure looked like he was going to kill him. A big fat lady away in the back of the theater couldn't stand it. She jumped up and squalled, "Look out! He's right there behind that big rock!"

Maybe things are better now, but I doubt it. I liked the fellow who plays Baretta a lot better when he was a little breech-clouted Indian chasing around after Red Ryder back in the not-too-distant times, when a woman didn't have to be naked to prove she was one, and a man didn't have to whip women and spew vulgarities to show he was tough.

Johnny Mac Brown, where are you?

'It was so touching that I almost wished I was dead'

Local Youth Killed on Arizona Mountain

You folks who have never spent much time in a high mountain country probably never gave much thought to rock rolling.

Don't laugh. It's quite a sport, and to be good at it, one must develop intricate skills of trajectory, time in motion equations, and the pure science of rockology.

A sheer bluff won't do. Anybody can drop something over a precipice, and nothing much happens when you do. Unless you're big on dull thuds and splashes, there is little pleasure in this.

What you need is a long, steep slope, with lots of other rocks and maybe some trees to knock down.

Moving targets, such as hikers, are great fun, but you'd be surprised at the lack of humor some people exhibit.

If you've ever read Zane Grey, you might recall that he, too, was a rock roller. He liked for his heroes to roll big rocks down on Mormons, the way Lassiter did in "Riders of the Purple Sage".

It was this Lassiter fellow who inspired me to roll rocks when he told Jane Witherspoon that he'd loved to roll rocks all his life, and now that he really wanted to roll a big one on some Mormons they were both mad at, he couldn't do it.

But, of course, he did.

The Mormons didn't like it much, but it inspired me to go to Arizona and roll a rock or two, which I did.

I convinced Middle Brother and a mutual friend of ours that life would be forever empty if we didn't go to Arizona, and we went.

My first rock rolling took place high up on the south slope of Superstition Mountain. A rock as big as your living room will bounce 30 or 40 feet high and jump the length of a football field when it gets going down a good mountain, and my first one was a beaut. It started an avalanche that must have hung dust 500 feet in the air. The rock itself rumbled clear out of sight. The last I saw of it, it looked like it was on its way to Tucson.

As the day progressed, I became separated from my companions; I had started down the mountain, and I thought they were following a short distance behind. I was belly up on my hands and feet, waddling feet first down a steep rock face when I heard a big rock coming, whump, whump, whump, down the mountain. In just a second or two, it came into view and it was quite plain that it and I were on a collision course. There was a low bluff just to my left and I managed to roll into its shelter just before the rock shattered the place where I had been like gravel does a windshield.

When the noise of the rock faded away, I heard Middle Brother and our friend calling me. You can bet I was plenty mad and I wouldn't answer. I just lay there under that little bluff and got madder.

They kept calling and pretty soon I could see them about 50 feet apart picking their way down through the rocks. It was plain that they were searching for my body.

They came on like that, calling and searching and sniffling a little bit, until they came together at the base of the slope just under me, where they sat down to rest.

I heard my brother say, "He was as good a brother as anybody ever had."

Our friend said, "I know it. Me and him was almost like brothers. I wisht we had a'been."

These boys had never talked like that about me before, and I began to soften a little toward them.

My brother said, "Me and him been lotsa miles together."

"He sure would do to ride the river with," said our friend.

And they both just boo hooed.

Pretty soon they had me crying along with them. It was so touching that I almost wished I was dead.

I pictured them carrying my mangled corpse down the mountain, and I made up a lead story for the Eastland Telegram that carried my picture and headlined, "Local Youth Killed on Arizona Mountain."

I got so involved in my sadness that our friend heard me blubbering, which was a neat piece of audio detection, considering all the slobbering they were doing.

"Shhhhh!" he whispered, "I think I hear 'im moanin! Listen!"

And they both jumped up and began looking around wild eyed in all the wrong directions.

It kind of irritated me the way they had cut off my noble demise. I had a rifle with me, an old British Enfield that had a voice like a howitzer, and I stuck it out over their heads and pulled off a round.

I never was sure whether they fainted or whether they both fell down trying to run.

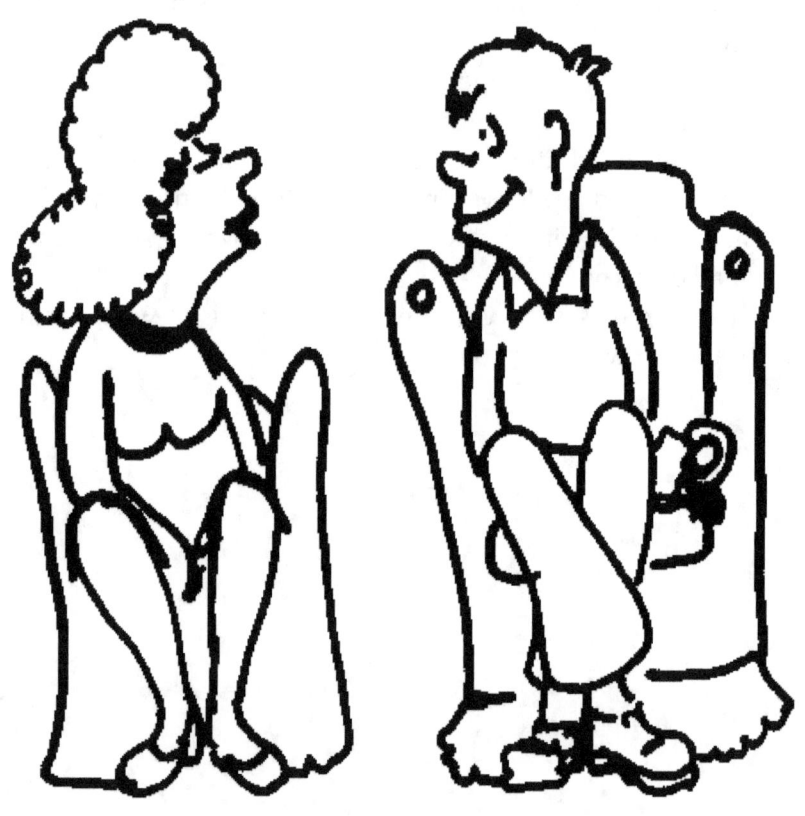

"When dey ain't lookin', you pour dat rotten coffee down inter dis big cushioney chair."

Of Hung Dogs
and Rotten Coffee

We didn't have any Cajuns on the headwaters of the Leon, so I got to be a grown man without knowing what one was, and I had it in my mind that Cajuns and Frenchmen were about the same thing. That was before I met my first Cajun, and he was kind enough to explain the difference to me about the third time I called him monsieur.

His name was Veazy. He was bigger than the law should allow to run around loose, and he said he lived on some bayou in South Louisiana that had an unpronounceable name that meant "tail of a turtle."

Veazy never would've left the tail of a turtle and I never would've left the headwaters of the Leon if the army hadn't invited us both to the same party.

One day they took about 200 of us out to where they had built some bleachers that you couldn't see a thing from and right after we all got set down, they told us to all stand up and drop our pants. I was a little bit uneasy about what they had on their minds, but I did like everybody else, and then they told us to all sit down again. When we had done that, they passed out a bunch of little tubes with wicked-looking needles built onto one end. They said we'd just been gassed and the only way to save our lives was to stick those needles in our thighs and squeeze in whatever it was in the tubes.

Well, it just goes against human nature to stab yourself, and I don't think some of those fellows believed we had actually been gassed at all. Everybody was approaching the thing as they thought best, and it was a pretty good show considering the talent present. Some of them would put the needle right against their leg and try to ease it in. Others figured the best way to do was to draw way back and run it home with one quick jab, but most of the time they would manage to get stopped just at the last.

Veazy was in a class all by himself. He went into a trance. His eyes glazed over and he went to machine-gunning his leg with the needle. Pretty soon he was slinging blood everywhere and getting faster as he went. It took a whole crowd of NCOs to get him stopped, and he stabbed two or three of them.

Veazy had been in the habit of slipping off every night to visit the local canteens, but his crippled leg kept him around the barracks for awhile. One night he came up to me and stared at me for several minutes. Then he asked me if I had ever hung a dog.

"No, Veazy," I said, "I never did. Do I look like somebody that would hang a dog?"

"Oh, yah," he assured me, "you do. I had a frand back home what looked a lot lak you, and he were de hangest dog feller in four or tree parishes. Me an him hung lots o' dogs."

"How come you'd do that?" I asked.

"Why," he said, "dey weren't annuder ting to do but hang dogs an hunt possums. Some nights we would do bof."

"You mean to tell me you'd hang your own possum dogs?" I asked.

"Well, not our good uns," he said, offended.

After that, for reasons known only to himself, Veazy would often impart bits and pieces of his wisdom to me. He gave me some social advice once that I've always meant to put to use.

He asked me if I'd know what to do if I ever went to somebody's house and the coffee was too horrible to drink. I asked him what, and he said, "It be plumb simple. Guests always gits de biggest an softest chair in de house, rat? Wal, when dey ain't lookin', you pour dat rotten coffee down inter dis big cushioney chair. Dey won't never know. I've did it lots o' times. An if it hoppen so dey is a sprang a-stickin' up out o' dis chair, you pour rat inter de spring, lak a funnel. Dat way, it don't leave no wet spot on de chair."

I never saw Veazy anymore after basic. But every time the coffee tastes bad, I think of him.

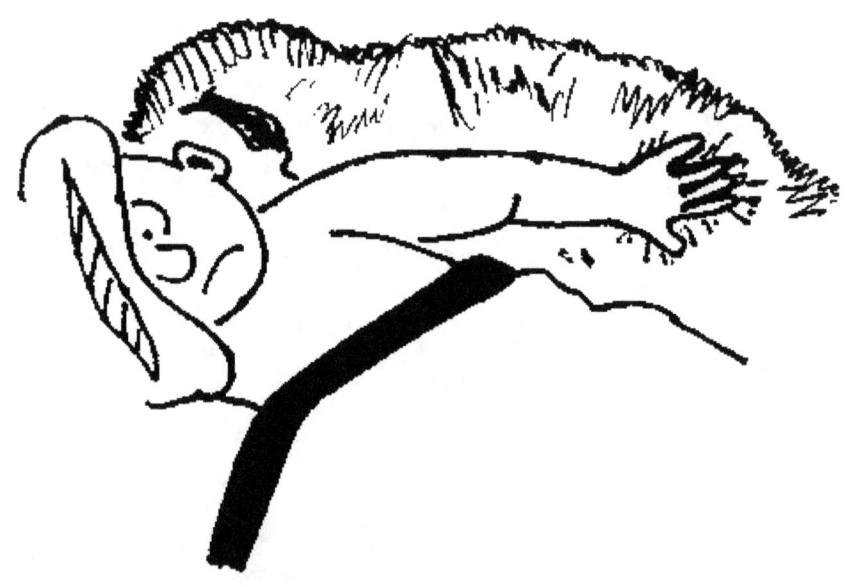

'It came to him that something was terribly wrong'

Scared Crazy

Ever wonder if there wasn't some lie you could tell or some act you could put on that would save you when the highway patrol catches you speeding?

Well now there is one. It existed all along, and only needed some daring genius to implement it.

I know a fellow who, caught cruising along at 80, was struck by inspiration when his eyes fell on a roll of toilet paper lying in the floor of his car, remnant of a recent picnic. Instead of slowing down, he increased his speed, and raced down the highway until he saw a likely looking clump of trees off in the pasture. Then he slammed on his brakes and came to a sliding stop in a shower of rocks and dust. He quickly grabbed the toilet paper, leaped over the fence and headed for the trees at a dead run, waving the toilet paper over his head as he went. The patrolman, convinced that he had encountered a true emergency, turned off his lights and kept going.

The man who told that story - we'll call him Bill - had another adventure one time that didn't come out quite as well.

Bill had a brother, Jack, who slept in the same bed with him when they were boys. Bill came in one night and went to sleep. Jack came in sometime later, wrapped himself up in an old deer hide, and crawled into bed with Bill. He nudged Bill until he had him awake enough to know something was in bed with him. He started to roll over, still not good awake, and in the process threw his arm over Jack's hairy form. He cautiously felt all that hair, and it came to him that something was terribly wrong. About that time Jack gave a little growl. Bill jumped out of bed, ran into a corner and commenced screaming at the top of his lungs. Jack, anxious to stop the racket, rolled out of the deer hide and turned on the light.

It was no use; Bill was locked into screaming and couldn't stop.

Their parents rushed into the room, and Jack told them what had happened. Bill was still up against the wall and they couldn't make him hush.

"Looky there what you've done," wailed their father, "You've scared Bill plumb out of his mind. He'll probably be crazy the rest of his life." Then he went to whipping Jack for scaring Bill crazy. Bill just stood there and screamed and watched the show.

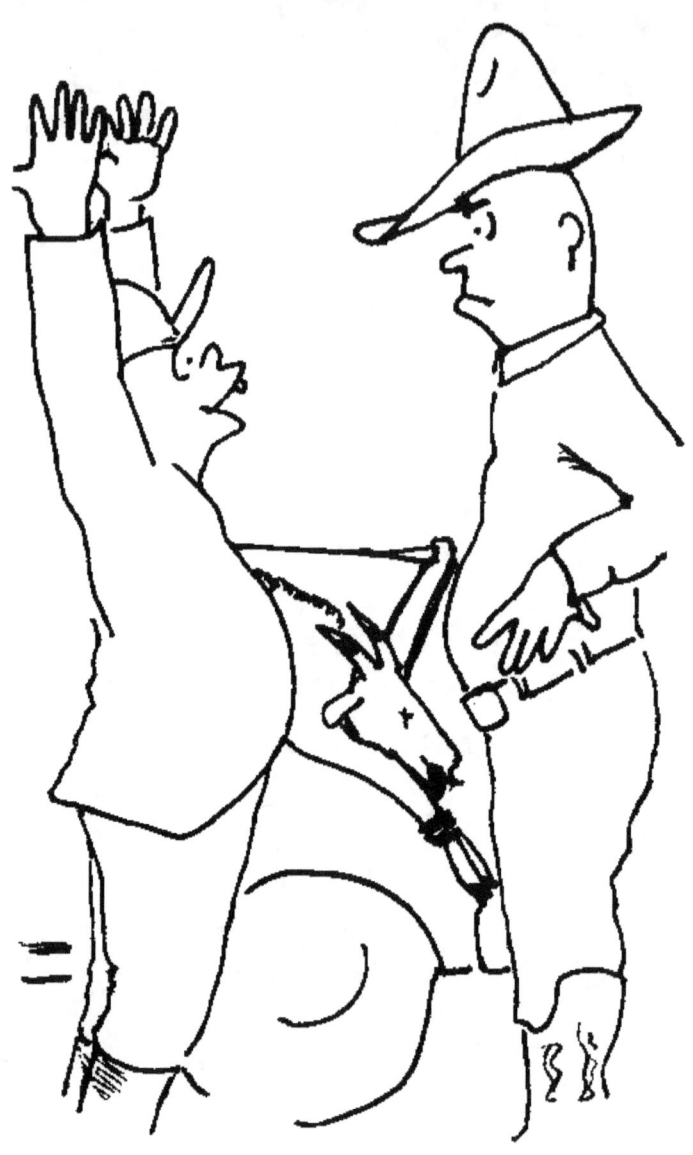

"It's an ALBINO SPIKE BUCK!"

The Albino Spike Buck

Before we know it, another deer season will be upon us, complete with rocking chair antler stories, missed shot because tales, and one time my uncle legends.

Everybody has a deer story. My favorite is one I witnessed years ago in Ranger. In those days, there was still a liberal sprinkling of cars from the 40's that had fenders a man could haul in his kill on, and just about everybody did so.

First you wallowed your deer all over the front of your car so as to spread a lot of blood around for effect. Then you used up the lengths of three or four lariats to tie him down.

Most cars had a hood ornament you could get a rope through or around, and you could use this to tie his head up high against the hood so everybody could see his horns.

Then, when you rolled into town, you started honking your horn. This was so you wouldn't have to wait around for a crowd to gather. Even people who didn't like you, and mostly hoped you'd shot yourself, would come out to look, on the chance that you'd gut-shot him or done something else they could make fun of.

Leasing to nonresident hunters was still mostly a new thing at that time in the Palo Pinto country, and the big city hunters, who were almost as goofy then as they are now, were a real treat to the locals.

Ranchmen used to argue about who had the dumbest hunters.

I happened to be in town one day when a ranchman from Keechi Creek won that year's argument.

You could generally hear a '47 Chevrolet coming quite awhile before you could see it coming, even if it's horn wasn't blaring, and the hunter who came flying in that morning was doing plenty of honking. Every little bit he'd stick his head out the window and holler.

From the racket he was making, we all figured he'd killed a bear or something. When he bounced into view, nobody there could believe what he had tied to his fender.

As fate would have it, the fellow who owned the land this kill had been made on was on the street. When the hunter spied him, he wheeled in right there and parked. Everybody hurried to get up close because they sure didn't want to miss any of the dialogue.

The hunter jumped out, just grinning all over, and hurried around to his trophy.

The ranchman, sensing a victory of rare proportions, waited until everybody got there and fell quiet before he said a word.

"What you got there?" he then asked pleasantly.

"What have I got?" jabbered the hunter, "Never seen one before, huh?"

He giggled and slobbered a little bit.

"I couldn't believe it at first myself."

He threw up his hands and shouted, "Why, man, it's an ALBINO SPIKE BUCK! And that ain't all! There musta been 50 in the bunch and they came right up to where I was hiding in the bushes! I wounded two or three of them, and if I hadn't run out of bullets, I could've gotten them, too!"

Hair goats didn't cost as much then as they do now, but when that Keechi Creek ranchman got to thinking about his hunter blasting away at a whole herd with a deer rifle, he decided it wasn't anywhere near as funny as some of us thought it was.

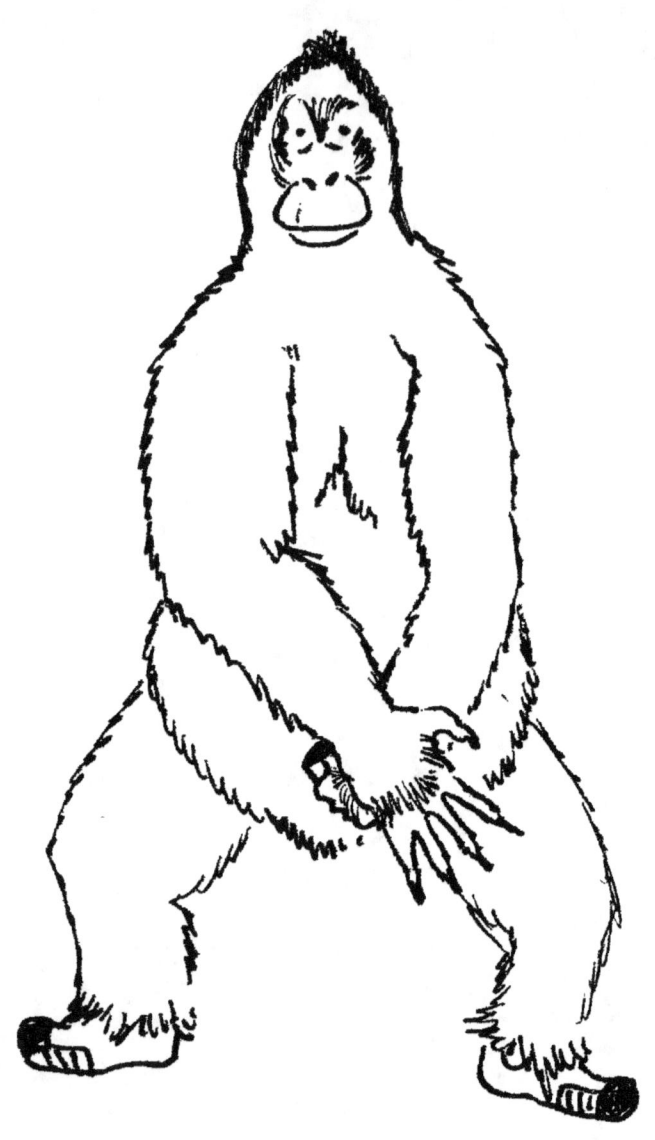

'I was known as the Caddo Critter'

Personal to the Milam County Monster

Every now and then, a monster shows up somewhere in the country. I was well acquainted with one of these fellows, called the Caddo Critter, and he sent the following letter through me to a younger monster over in East Texas who called himself the Milam County Monster.

Dear Milam,

You may not remember me, but I was in the monster business a long time before you ever stuck your smelly face out of the brush, and I thought perhaps I could sort of help you along your way, and possibly save your life.

Back in my time, which fell roughly between the second Lake Worth Monster and the Haskell Thang, I was known as the Caddo Critter.

Like you, I was a gorilla type monster. Unlike you, I did not indulge in tracks. People love finding those tracks, Milam, but they can get you exposed as a fake, which, as you know, is the last thing any real faker wants.

The problem lies in the engineering; you just can't make an authentic looking giant track, and any animal expert in the country will know the difference. So lay off the tracks, especially now that you have everybody's undivided attention. Those folks are armed and dangerous now, Milam, and they will most assuredly blow your head off if you come out to make more tracks.

I congratulate you on your foul odor. I freely admit that such never occurred to me during my active career, and I have no idea how you are doing it, unless you really do stink on your own.

I hate being so negative about your performance, but you should have known better than to try chasing that boy. I know, and you must by now realize, that the gorilla mask impairs your vision, especially downward.

You are absolutely the first major monster ever known to have fallen on his can while on active duty. It detracts from the dignity of us all, Milam, and I herewith reprimand you for it.

I'm going to offer you some advice that the rest of us learned the hard way, and I sincerely hope that you will heed it, and save some problems for us all:

1. You've done enough. Every nut in East Texas plus some imported maniacs who saw "The Creature from Black Lake," or "The Monster of Boggy Creek," are armed to the teeth and out there creeping through the woods. They are already frightened, and they will blast anything that moves (the posse that was after me shot 14 hair goats that first night).

Let the imaginers and the liars run the show from here. They will think of things you never would have and they will give you greater mobility - you can be seen in three or four places at once.

2. Never admit your true identity. I know this is hard, Milam, not taking credit for your act, but there are reasons.

For example, there was a fellow who was a pretty good friend of mine. He was newly wed, and had a little ranch house on the lip of the canyon I chose as the den area of the Caddo Critter. His wife told him he could either live on the canyon alone, or somewhere else with her. He now hates me.

Then there was this girl who said the Critter chased her until she hung her dress in a barbed wire fence, at which time, she said, it caught her and did things unbecoming man or monster. You can see, Milam, that if people believe such things, they might send you away. You could even be tried twice, once as a man and once as a monster.

If you will forward me your name in utmost secrecy, I will recommend you for membership in BOOGER (Bonded Organization Of Outrageous Gentlemen for Environmental Rampages).

As a member, you will meet the California Bigfoot, the Wolf Girl of Devil's River, the Boggy Creek Monster, and many, many more (sorry, you won't be able to meet the Haskel Thang - turned out he was a real varmint. Happens in the best of clubs).

Caddo

"I have to move the boards around
every onct in awhile"

The All-Weather Farm

Lying Mac always told that he had a farm somewhere away over in East Texas. He'd disappear sometimes for three or four days and when he'd show up again, he'd always say that he'd been to check on his farm. We all thought it was kind of odd, him having that nice, 500 acre farm over there in East Texas when he never owned anything more than the shirt on his back around Hog Town, where he was born, raised, and stayed.

When he first invented this farm, he was always bragging about how much rain fell on it because Hog Town, you see, is always more of less in a drought except when Hog Creek overflows and washes everything away. He just couldn't find words to explain how that farm of his never suffered for water.

"The ground is so moist," he said, "that you can stomp yer foot and the ground will quiver like jello fer fifty acres around."

Another time he said, "Ye know, boys, they is a few drawbacks to ownin' land in the rain belt. I had a kind of problem with my cows a-boggin' down, but I solved it alright. I laid boards end to end all around over the pasture and bless me if them old cows didn't learn right off how to walk on the boards and graze along either side. I have to move the boards around every onct in awhile, but that way I kin rest part of my pasture all the time."

Everybody put up with Mac's wonderful farm for years. Then we had a sure-enough bad drought - a real, old time, dryup - and that drought put Mac and his wet weather farm out of business. Why, we had drought cracks out in the Leon Bottoms that you could throw an East Texas farm off into, and we had waterholes to dry up that nobody had ever been able to find bottom before, much less look at. Mac's board walking cows were no match at all for the monster catfish, skeletons, and old Spanish cannons that were turning up at the bottom of those waterholes.

Mac finally couldn't stand it anymore and he just disappeared. Nobody saw hide nor hair of him for the better part of a week. When he finally did show up, the drought had got to his farm.

"Boys," he said, "I sure hated to jis up and go like I done without a word to nobody, but, ye see, I got a emergency call from my ranch foreman over in East Texas. This here drought had spread over to there without my knowin' about it and my cows was a-dyin' o' thirst. I had to go quick and see what I could do, and I tell ye right now, boys, I like not to a-made 'er. I left Hog Town a-runnin' wide open and never looked back. Somewhere tother side o' Dallas, I went to sleep at the wheel and hit a curb. Boys, I flipped 'er nine times end over end in the air, come down on my wheels, and never let off on 'er."

Booger Barnes, said, "Mac, how in the world could ye tell how many times ye flipped? Was ye a-countin' 'em?"

Mac said, "Yes, Booger, I did count the flips. Funny how a man's mind works at a time like 'at." And he went right on with his story.

"Well, sir," he said, "I pulled into my pasture jist about daylight, and my pore old cows seen me and come a-staggerin' up to the gate, lookin' to me to do sompum fer 'em. 'Old cows,' I says, 'ole Mac'll do what 'e kin.' But I tell ye, boys, she was the worst I ever seen, bar none. The dust come up around my feet so thick I could barely see to walk around. I'd allus heered tell that ye could sometimes find water by diggin' in a dry streambed, so not knowin' what else to do, I drug a cane pole outa the back of my car and went to pokin' around in the creekbed with them pore old cows a-follerin' me around like dyin' kittens. I 'as jist ready to give 'er up when, WHOOSH! All of a sudden a big stream o' water come ashootin' outa the ground, and I ain't never seen that cane pole til yet."

He paused and help up one hand with his fingers spread wide, letting all those droughted-out farmers have visions of that gushing stream of water.

Then he said, "Boys, I'll kiss yer foot if they ain't a ten acre lake there right this minute."

Buck Miller walker over to his pickup, reached in, got a cane pole, and stuck it in Mac's hand. "Mac," he said, "They's about fourteen jillion dry creekbeds between here and the county line. You jist spend the rest of the day a-pokin' in 'em."

'If they were afraid something was spoiled, or poisoned
I was called in as professional consultant'

The Speech Lesson

A long time ago, in the innocence of being very young, I was considerably put upon and consistently taken advantage of by two older brothers and one older sister. I personally took advantage of no one, for, when my parents viewed me, and saw what they had done, they went out of the production business.

The only things around the house younger than me were Big Jersey's calf, some of the chickens, and Chatterbox the squirrel.

If Older Brother whipped Middle Brother, it was certain that Little Brother would, just to keep the chain unbroken, be promptly thrashed by Middle Brother.

if something turned up lost or broken, I was blamed and punished. They started out doing it before I was old enough to talk, at which time they assumed my guilt by virtue of nolo contendere. After I became vocal, they figured I had learned to lie to avoid whippings, and whipped me once for the crime, and again for lying.

If they were afraid something was spoiled, or poisoned, I was called in as professional consultant. That is, they would feed it to me. If I spit it out, they would grab it up and dispose of it, so the dog wouldn't eat it and die.

If I could get it down, they would watch me for an hour or two, and if I didn't get sick, they would eat the rest of it.

Middle Brother had a thing with certain words. For instance, he could, when not excited, say 'star' and 'mother', but he was convinced that the true words were 'shar' and 'nuhnuh', and when he was excited, he couldn't say much of anything right.

He also spelled our name with a 't' on the end. Nobody could convince him it was wrong. It was, he said, his name, and he could spell it however he wanted to, and he definitely wanted to put a 't' at the end.

I was trusting, and I believed Middle Brother. He convinced me to say shar and nuhnuh, and he was teaching me to write my name with a 't' on the end.

Older Brother and Sister held a conference. It was embarrassing, they decided, to have a brother in the second grade who said shar and nuhnuh and desecrated the family name with that ever-present 't'. Besides which, he was teaching Little Brother, who was already an idiot, and a criminal, his disgusting habits.

Drastic action was called for.

On a day when both parents were gone and school was out, they implemented their plan.

Sister was the official executioner in the absence of Mother. All whippings were administered with razor straps. Under normal conditions, if the offense was not of too serious a nature, the transgressor had the option of choosing which strap he was to be beaten with. Nobody ever chose a certain super-thick, extra long strap that looked like a holdover from the inquisition, but on this particular day, Sister appeared with this formidable weapon in her hand. Older Brother was with her with another strap.

They herded us into the dining room, where we saw a chocolate cake and two glasses of cool milk on the table.

"We are about to whip you," announced Sister. "Until you say star and mother and admit that there is no 't' at the end of our name. When you do, you can have cake and milk."

Thereupon, they applied the leather.

About the third lick, I squalled, "MOTHERSTAR-NO-T" and headed for the cake, but they had Middle Brother excited.

"SHAR," he screamed, "NUHNUH!"

I had worked the cake over pretty well before they gave out and gave up without even getting him to deny the 't'.

I am proud to report, though, that today he says star and mother just as plain as Dale Carnegie, and he never again was known to spell his name with a 't'. He did not, however, get any cake. Nobody did but me, for what I had not eaten, I had played with.

Middle Brother and I had made our headquarters on the back porch roof. He called a conference one day and said to me, "We got to quit cussin'. If we don't we're gonna go to hell, sure as anything."

Actually I had never cussed, but once and that was by accident. I had never thought about going to hell, but I figured it wouldn't be any fun without Middle Brother, and he didn't act much like he wanted to go. So I said, "How we gonna stop?"

He had thought it all out.

"I'll tell you," he said, "what we'll do is, we'll take turns sayin' all the cuss words we know. Then, see, we'll have it all out of our systems, and we can forget about it."

I didn't know but two words that he considered as actually cussing, so it didn't take long to finish.

He said he sure felt a lot better about it, now that neither of us was going to hell, and I said I did too.

I must tell you, though, that Middle Brother did not keep the bargain for long. And when I reminded him that he was probably going to hell, he punched me in the nose.

I got a red wagon for Christmas when I just turned five, direct from Santa Claus, and it was, to me, the greatest piece of machinery ever invented. Middle Brother liked it passably well himself, which was fine, because it takes two to really have fun with a wagon.

We tried a few little slopes with the tongue held back to steer with, and it was lots of fun.

Older Brother observed us at this game, and found us a really good hill, plenty steep and awfully high looking to a five-year-old.

Evidently it looked pretty high to both brothers too, because nobody wanted to try it. For them, however, the problem was not a serious one.

Older Brother came over to me and said, "Get in the wagon and I'll shove you around."

"Oh boy," I said, "Will you shove me real fast?"

"Oh yes," he assured me, "I'll shove you faster than you've ever been."

He did too, right up to the edge of that steep slope, and right on over. I kept the wheels straight because I was petrified, and went straight to the bottom without a hitch.

When my brothers saw that I was alive and well, they confiscated my red wagon and that was the last ride I got until they grew tired of the game.

'He stabbed it to the hilt in Joe's massive belly'

Clyde Richard Stabs a Deacon

Clyde Richard decided one Sunday, after church that we really needed a peep-hole in the door of the primary Sunday School room. With all the secret stuff we had to plan, he said, we couldn't have people slipping up on us.

I didn't see how the peep-hole was going to do us as much good as it would anybody standing on the outside, but I thought it was a good idea anyway.

He took the first turn at the door, boring our hole with his pocket knife. He was really leaning into it, to get things started, when big, fat Joe Clark, one of the deacons, suddenly opened the door.

Clyde Richard fell through the doorway and into Joe Clark with his knife still in boring position. He stabbed it to the hilt in Joe's massive belly.

Joe Clark screamed and lit out.

Clyde Richard said, "He run off with my knife stickin' in 'im. I bet I don't never git it back."

My daddy was at the church that Sunday. Both he and Clyde Richard's daddy were in the same group of men, standing around talking in the churchyard.

We slipped out to where we could hear Joe Clark's report.

"I went back 'ere to check the lights," wailed Joe, "and when I opened the door, Clyde Richard and Leroy jumped out and stabbed me in the belly."

My daddy said, "You sure want to watch them 10-year-olds, Joe. They're sure dangerous."

"But they had knives," cried Joe, who weighed about 300 pounds. "Well," said my daddy, "One of 'em ain't got one no more. It's a' sticking in your belly."

Clyde Richard's daddy was starting to lead everybody in our direction, so we ran off and hid in the canyon.

The stabbing of Joe Clark, on top of all the other stuff Clyde Richard had done lately, had the whole church in an uproar. Strong measures were called for; Clyde Richard would have to deliver a testimonial of faith.

Like any true criminal, Clyde Richard knew just how far he could push, and he knew that he was going to have to give that testimonial or leave home.

I had given one not long before that caused some of the old ladies to speculate on my prospects as a future preacher, so we decided to change mine around and run it again as Clyde Richard's. He did the first honest work of his life trying to memorize that testimonial, and he had it down pat. He practiced until he could wave his arms and raise his voice at all the right places just like a regular preacher, and I heard him go over it so many times that I got to believing that he really meant it.

Clyde Richard had been impressed at some point in his life by the old maxim, "If at first you don't succeed, then try, try again." He had personalized it to fit his own peculiar style, and, since it was only a two-liner, he could always remember it, even when he couldn't remember anything else.

When his turn came on testimonial night, and he got behind the pulpit, with the notes he'd been memorizing all week laid out before him, I saw a look of terrible fear come over him. He opened his mouth a time or two, but nothing came out. His eyes glazed over and locked on empty space toward the back of the auditorium. Then he blurted out, "If at first you don't friends need, then fry, fry a hen."

Now that little quote didn't really mean anything at all to Clyde Richard, or even make good sense to him, and besides that, he didn't even know what he was saying at the time. But you'd be amazed at the long list of insults that a bunch of chicken eating Baptists could read into so few words.

'When he knocked the Allgood boys in the head
with his club, why, that was funny'

Booger Makes a Lawman

Back during The War, the government got real desperate and drafted Booger Barnes without knowing what they were doing.

They tested Booger a hundred different ways and he had to talk to some really weird people in little shut-up rooms where they asked him things like did he hate his mama, and showed him all sorts of things and asked him what did he think of when he saw them.

They finally turned him loose and made him an M.P., with a funny white cap and a long black club and a gun.

Booger came home on leave before they shipped him overseas and he wore his M.P. getup to Hog Town to show everybody. He told Buckshot Butts, the constable, that he was a federal officer and outranked him, and that he would run things while he was in town. Buckshot wasn't real sure about that, but he knew how Booger was, and that there wasn't a bit of use to call up to the county seat to find out if an M.P. private outranked a precinct constable, because Booger had done made up his mind and never would admit to anything different no matter who said it.

Booger made a passable lawman, only maybe he was a little too strict. When he knocked the Allgood boys in the head with his club for spitting on the sidewalk, why, that was funny; everybody but the Allgood boys said so. But when he arrested the Baptist preacher's wife for jaywalking, things got a little sticky.

When it first happened, there wasn't but two other grown men in town, besides Booger, that knew what jaywalking was, but they knew what "naked as a jaybird" was, and they thought maybe she had run across the street naked, and so got a pretty good rumor started about that.

The preacher we had then, Brother Bennie Spivey, was a reformed bootlegger that had had a vision one time that called him to the ministry. Back before the vision, Brother Bennie had been mean as a red hog, and everybody figured that he would kill Booger, then pray for forgiveness and a No Bill.

There wasn't any jailhouse in Hog Town, and Booger had the preacher's wife (she was a right pretty little thing.) under house arrest at Buckshot Butt's house. Buckshot wasn't liking it any, and him and Booger was hollering back and forth at one another. Sister Spivey was squalling something awful, and pretty near everybody in town had turned out to watch the show. Some of the old men were saying that it was a penitentiary offense to hit a preacher, same as it was to shoot a buzzard, and that Booger couldn't defend himself without going to jail for it.

Some good soul of course, probably a Methodist, went and got the preacher, and he came storming in like everything would be over just as soon as he got that door open and got ahold of Booger, but it never happened that way. Booger was laying for him, and when he yanked that door open and stuck his head in at it, Booger whapped that old long black club the army had given him longways between the preacher's eyes and laid him out in the yard stiff as a poker.

That was too much for the old folks, and they run off and called up to the county seat for the sheriff to come and shoot Booger Barnes for hitting a preacher.

Meanwhile, Brother Bennie came to himself, but he didn't seem to remember there for a while that he was an ordained Baptist preacher. He lit in to cussing something awful, and went tearing across the road to Junior Millican's filling station. Pretty soon he came running back with a can of gasoline and a pack of gopher matches, and said he was going to burn Booger out. Everybody went to reminding him that his wife was in there, and that besides that it was Buckshot Butts' house, but the preacher just kept on yelling and trying to get loose from the crowd so he could set fire to the house.

He would've done it, too, if the sheriff hadn't called one of his deputies that was close enough to get there about then. He took the matches and the gasoline away from Brother Bennie and hollered for Booger to come out of the house, and Booger had sense enough to do it, even though he never did admit that he wasn't the ranking officer of the law in town that day. The deputy hauled Brother Bennie and Booger off to the county seat, and we never seen Booger again until after The War. All they done, though, was put him on a train back to wherever it was he was supposed to be stationed.

Brother Bennie had kind of soiled his halo over the whole mess, and about half his congregation - fifteen or twenty people, counting the kids - quit him and started a new church. That cut the money down considerable, and pretty soon Brother Bennie throwed up his pulpit and went back to bootlegging. He sold Booger a half-pint of Old Crow the first day Booger was home after The War, and everything came out fine.

No artwork has survived
for Picasso and Possums

Go figure

Picasso and Possums

This fellow Picasso did some things to art that never were very deeply appreciated up on the headwaters of the Leon. At first, we thought those strange scribblings were some sort of pointless Yankee joke, and we never figured that there really was anybody named Picasso that had the gall to claim he was trying to sell them. When we found out it was for real, being open minded and tolerant, we set in to try and figure out the sense of it all.

Clyde Richard had this magazine that showed a bunch of Picasso's "works," and the one him and Sleeping Jesus Woodall selected for study was called "Nude Descending a Staircase." They picked that one because if she was really in there somewhere they wanted to see her, and because that was about the only one that claimed to have anything in it that they thought they might recognize.

Well, they studied that thing for the longest, and they found part of the staircase and bits and pieces of what might have been the girl, but it was hard to be sure of anything. They concluded that if the folks at the Metropolitan Museum of Fine Art in New York City thought that was a naked woman, then they ought to be able to fool them like Picasso had done, and get rich.

They were smart enough to know that their art had to be regional, something they knew all about, and that it had to be something they could give a fancy title to that told a little story by itself, like Picasso's "Nude Descending a Staircase." They got up thirty or forty plans and when they got done weeding out, they had picked one that we all felt certain was the best that could have been thought of. They called it "Possum Ascending a Persimmon Tree." Clyde Richard was elected to draw it since it all seemed simple enough, and since he said that he had figured out Picasso's style. First off, he said, Picasso had got about a second grader to draw his stuff so it wouldn't look too real. Then he had cut the drawing up like a jigsaw puzzle, only when he put it back together, he purposely put all the pieces in the wrong places. Well, that's how he done his "work," only instead of using a second grader, he got Sleeping Jesus to do it, which was about the same thing from a professional point of view.

He sent off his work to the Metropolitan Museum of Fine Art in New York City and sat down to wait for an answer. He thought they might just send a check without any letter or that they might demand that he come to New York City at once and draw a bunch of stuff while he was there. That scared him so bad that he got to wishing he never had of sent them his work in the first place, and after a day or two he was so upset with the thought of going off to New York City that he was afraid to look in his mail box.

After a week had gone by, he thought them high-falutin' folks in New York City must be awful slow. After two weeks, he thought they must have mighty poor manners. After three weeks, it came to him in the night that they wasn't going to buy his work or even tell them they wasn't going to do it. He jumped out of bed and opened that magazine up to "Nude Descending a Staircase" and studied it some more just to be fair about it, and to make real sure that "Possum Ascending a Persimmon Tree" really was a better looking picture. Satisfied, he throwed that magazine out the window and set right down and wrote this letter to the Metropolitan Museum of Fine Art in New York City.

"Dear Ignernt Fool in Charge: 3 weeks ago I sent you a picture called Possum Ascending a Persimmon Tree. Everthang in it was jist like as the nose on your dumb face until I turned it into modern art by shuffling thangs around a little bit. Anybody in Hog Town can tell you right off that they ain't nothin' worth knowin' about possums that I don't already

know, and I can tell you right now that I have studied Nude Descending a Staircase, and I know a whole lot more about possums than Picasso knows about nekkid women.

I have decided that I will not under any circumstances allow you to keep my picture any longer, and if you don't send it back right now, I am going to sue you for everything you have got in this world. I am going to donate Possum to a new museum we are starting up here in Hog Town (he made that part up), and you can watch cobwebs cover up Nude."

Well, he run down about daylight the next morning to get his letter in the earliest possible mail, and after he had made sure it was going air mail to New York City, he hung around town for a little while telling everybody what he'd done. Then he went on home, and lo and behold, there in his mailbox was one of those long, snow-white letters made special for the people that sent it, and this one was from the Metropolitan Museum of Fine Art in New York City.

It scared him so bad that he run all the way over to Sleeping Jesus' house before he even opened it up. Then the two of them opened it real careful like with a pocket knife. It read:

"Dear Sir:
We deeply regret that we are unable to place "Possum Ascending a Persimmon Tree"
In our display of fine art. Most of our art comes to us through the services of
Professional agents. We respectfully suggest that this method might prove best for
You."

To Clyde Richard, "we are unable to place" meant that they didn't have room on their walls. And that stuff about agents, why, that was as clear an invitation as anybody ever heard tell of!

But there was that awful letter he had sent off by air mail.

He burnt up a good Ford car getting back to Hog Town but it was too late; the letter was on its way and there wasn't a thing anybody could do about it. Clyde Richard had ruined his big chance of becoming a rich and famous artist.

He has told about how he could have had a picture hanging in the Metropolitan Museum of Fine Art in New York City so many times since then that some of the newcomers around Hog Town don't know any better. They even wrote him up in the county seat paper last year as "Hog Town's Unknown Master-The Man Who Could Have Been Picasso." They told all about how he had invented the modern art style that had made Picasso famous and how Picasso had copied his technique of giving his pictures names like "Nude Descending a Staircase." When the original works from Hog Town had arrived, the article said, Picasso had run ahead of him and had covered all the walls with his stuff so that there wasn't any more room, and Clyde Richard had "come home in disgust, through forever with the devious world of glittering lights and fame."

I expect that when he dies, they'll put up one of those 'near here' historical markers out where him and Sleeping Jesus Woodall created "Possum Ascending a Persimmon Tree." The newspaper article, though, just said he painted scenes of native wildlife. It never mentioned possums at all.

"Are you hurt, Raymond?"

The Coon Tail Conflict

When I was a Sophomore in high school, a new boy moved into our town.

He was a big old tall, gangling boy, about 6' 4", but his coordination hadn't caught up with his growth yet.

My brother Raymond and I were the only boys in town who kept hounds and sold hides in the winter. We had a little pencil-tailed hound named Lady that we were extra proud of.

This new boy, Ronald, found out about our hound, and announced that he was an expert coon hunter. He said he would be glad to show us how it was done.

That announcement was not one that made us very proud of our new acquaintance. We were under the impression that we were already pretty good hunters.

Ronald inspected our dog, and said she sure wasn't much to look at, which was true, but which we didn't care to be told.

He said his buddy's dog back in Abilene, Old Rowdy, was a much better looking dog, and he imagined that old Rowdy was in fact a better dog.

He had unending tales of Old Rowdy picking up days old trails and treeing unheard-of numbers of coons.

We hated Old Rowdy.

We were kind-hearted boys and we let Ronald go hunting with us (actually, we thought maybe we could lose him or kill him).

He showed up for the first hunt wearing a carbide lamp on his head.

We had never seen one before.

Ronald told us it was the only thing to use. His buddy back in Abilene wouldn't use anything else.

We hated his buddy back in Abilene.

119

Lady ran over a coon and treed him before we could get away from the car, which pleased us immensely and caused us to act as though it happened all the time.

It was winter, and we always shot coons in winter so the dogs wouldn't tear the hides.

Raymond had the only gun, and for some reason he missed the first three shots.

Ronald began making fun of him. He allowed that anybody ought to be able to hit that coon.

Now, Raymond actually had a sense of humor, but you sort of had to know him pretty well to realize it.

Ronald didn't know him very well.

He missed the fourth shot, and Ronald laughed out big and loud.

Raymond said, "I'll tell you what, Ronald, I'm a little better at moving targets. If you'll take off running, I'll be glad to shoot you."

Ronald didn't say anything, and Raymond stood there looking at him like he was waiting.

Ronald edged over to me and said, "Does he really mean that?"

"Oh yes," I said. "Go ahead, he won't make you run very far."

That didn't seem to appeal to Ronald. He sat down on a big log and got quiet.

Raymond finally got tired of putting the mean eye on him, since Ronald couldn't see his expression very well anyway with his carbide lamp, and shot the coon out.

We started on down the river, and didn't get far before Ronald fell over a log. His carbide lamp blew up when he hit the ground. It made a big noise and flash and Ronald lay perfectly still.

Raymond had been a short distance ahead. He raced back and said, "Did it kill him?"

I shined my light on him. He blinked at me. I could see that all of his head was still there, though part of his hair was singed back to the scalp.

"Naw," I said, "I don't think he's even hurt."

"Heck," said my brother, and started off down the river again.

Lady treed the second time up a tall, dead elm that was standing right on the bluff of the river bank. We could see a hollow about 35 feet off the ground, and knew the coon was in it.

Raymond climbed up to see how deep the hollow was, and what we would have to do to get the coon out.

The tree had been dead for a long time, and its roots had rotted. It popped and groaned a little as Raymond climbed, but those old river bottom trees are usually fairly steady for years and years after they die and we didn't think much about it.

He reached the hollow and shined his light into it. He was standing on a limb on the river side of the tree. He raised up and said he could see the coon.

Just at that point the tree gave a single, loud pop, and started over.

There was nothing Raymond could do but stand up there big-eyed and ride it down.

It would've been spectacular enough just falling, but the river bank was about 15 or 20 feet high, and it fell off it. There was only a little water in the river and it was pooled against the far bank, leaving the wreck to happen on a gravel bar.

Limbs as big as my body broke off and went flying through the air. The dust was so thick that I couldn't find Raymond for several seconds. When I did, he was lying on his back with his eyes closed and was half buried in broken limbs.

I thought sure he was dead.

Ronald galloped up and said, "Are you hurt, Raymond?"

Raymond opened one eye and looked at him.

"Why hell no, Ronald," he said, "I probably didn't fall over a hundred feet. Why would I be hurt?"

Then he said to me, "Give me the gun. I'm gonna shoot this idiot," and I knew he was alright.

He'd kept close to the trunk, and the limbs on that side had cushioned his fall.

He never did shoot Ronald, even though I did give him the gun, and Ronald liked to hunt so much that he kept going with us after that night.

Everybody around school decided that even though Ronald was big, he wasn't too war-like. And after Jack Hilliard hit him in the head with a basketball and knocked him cold as a cucumber, his reputation was pretty well shot. We played dodge-ball all the time, and nobody had ever been knocked out before.

It got to be an embarrassment to us that Ronald was known to hunt with us. So I was glad when he unexpectedly proved himself.

It happened in the neighboring town of Gordon, where we had gone to play basketball.

Ronald had a collection of coon tails that he'd brought with him from Abilene, and he was so taken with his role as a coon hunter that he carried the things around in his pocket everywhere he went.

He played on the B team, but our coach always let the B team suit up for games.

That night, during the girl's game, we saw a big old rough-looking boy from Gordon go up into the little cubbyhole they'd let us dress in. He came out after a few minutes and sat down in a chair on the stage, which was at one end of the basketball court.

We thought he might've taken something, and Ronald went to investigate.

He soon came tearing out, wild-eyed and ran up to the Gordon boy and grabbed him up by the collar.

It was a small gym, and everybody on and off the court got quiet to watch what was happening.

Ronald yelled out, "Where's my coon tails?"

The other fellow couldn't seem to grasp the situation,

"Your what?" he gasped.

"My - - - - coon tails," screamed Ronald.

"I don't know," confessed the Gordon boy, "Turn me loose."

"Not till I find my coon tails," hollered Ronald, and he began pounding on the supposed thief.

School authorities broke the fight up before it got far, and our school had to make a formal apology for what became known as the Coon Tail Conflict.

It turned out that, for once, Ronald had left his coon tails at home. Our superintendent suggested that he do so permanently.

We got to like Ronald so much that when he borrowed Old Rowdy for a weekend, and Lady treed 5 coons to his none, and Rowdy took the wrong end of a trail twice, we felt bad about it.

'This baby ghost used to emerge from the chimney every night and walk back and forth along the comb of the house making ghostly sounds'

Ghosts and Other Boogers

Most people who believe in ghosts have seen one, and vice-versa.

I never did.

I was even in a car with five other people who swore they did, and I didn't.

We had, as everybody does, a haunted house by a cemetery where I grew up, complete with a spooky river bottom. That's where the other five saw the ghost that I didn't.

My cousin Arthur, who rode a big white horse and was known as the Lone Ranger, says a 'light' chased him several miles one night. He said Old Silver saw it too, and wanted to run, so he let him. Old Silver jumped a creek he ordinarily couldn't clear in three jumps, and the light stopped on the other side.

There was a famous baby ghost in an old house near Double Mountain in Stonewall County. The story was that a baby had been killed in the house, and this baby ghost used to emerge from the chimney every night and walk back and forth along the comb of the house making ghostly sounds.

A young fellow in the neighborhood spread the word that on a certain night he was going to shoot the ghost off the house. A big crowd gathered to see him do it, and right on cue, the ghost stepped from the chimney and started down the rooftop. The young cowboy threw up his rifle and fired. The ghost came tumbling down as women screamed and fainted. Turned out the ghost was a hoot owl.

Another fellow I know moved into a haunted house where a mass murder had taken place during a hard norther. Every time the wind shifted to the north, the ghosts of the murdered

125

people would go to howling, but they quit after he removed a half-buried Mason jar that faced north from under the house.

A couple of old time Texians, Creed Taylor and Big Foot Wallace teamed up to give this country it's best authentic ghost in the form of a headless horseman.

Down in the brush country they trailed a band of Mexican horse thieves to ground and killed them all. Wallace had a flair for practical jokes, and Taylor wasn't exactly finicky. They cut off the head of the bandit leader, tied it into his sombrero, strapped the sombrero to his body, and lashed the dead man to the saddle of a half-wild mustang. They stuck a pole up under the corpse's clothing so he could sit up and turned the mustang loose.

The poor horse could not thereafter approach other horses without stampeding them, and was soon half-crazy. A great many people said they saw the Headless Horseman. Some of them shot it, without, of course, any effect.

It's fame grew, and Wallace and Taylor kept quiet. The mystery was finally solved when an enterprising cowboy shot the horse.

The citizens, however were not ready to part with their favorite spook, and they kept right on seeing him. Some even claimed to have held ghostly conversations with him.

Folks hunger for such things. They want - they demand - that something be out there in the dark. Wouldn't it be a sorry world without ghosts and monsters and things that go bump in the night?

'Mac settled back on the top step of the bank,
where he had been all morning long'

Great Liars I Have Known

I have been blessed in my lifetime, for I have personally known at least four world class liars. The greatest of these was Lying Mac. He was never beaten, and never forced to retraction, no matter how outrageous his lie, and let's face it, anybody can lie about common things that sound reasonable. Mac possessed all the characteristics of a champion in his chosen field; he could instantly lie on any subject known to man, and he could string one lie smoothly into another on a totally different subject without leaving any rough edges. Mac's dexterity was a wondrous thing. You could never even begin to guess in which direction his imagination would next leap.

One day, for example, Mac said, right out of the blue, "My first old lady was the daughter of the prime minister of Saskatchewan."

"Why, Mac, how come you didn't stay up there where ye had some pull?" asked Claudie Shodgrass.

"Old lady didn't like the climate," said Mac, instantly.

"What was ye doin' in Saskatchewan, anyways?" asked One Eye Daniels, winking at me. (The only way you could tell whether One Eye was asleep or winking was to listen and see if he was snoring.).

"I was puttin' up radio signal towers for the gummint," said Mac.

Nobody said anything for a minute, and Mac got uneasy that he was going to lose his audience, so he added, offhand like, "They had plenty of folks up there that could put up radio towers, mind ye, but, the thang is, they didn't have nobody that knowed how to install high level classified relays."

Mac rubbed his chin, and spit, and made like he was about to get up and walk off. Then he gave a little chuckle, and said, "Wouldn't none of 'em climb that high even if they had knowed what to do when they got there."

"How high did ye have to climb?" bit Sleeping Jesus Allgood.

Mac settled back on the top step of the bank, where he had been all morning long, and said, "Well, boys, she varied quite a bit, but the highest tower I ever clumb was 12,473 foot high to the bottom of the main span. That's what we called the holding device for the top lights and the high level classified relays. Hit was fifty-six more plumb up to the top where I had to go."

"What's a high level classified relay?" asked Claudie.

Mac just snickered and wiped snuff off his mouth with the back of his hand. "Why, I cain't tell ye that, Claudie. Hit would violate my top secret clearance with the gummint. All I can say is, they's very technical army equipment."

"Didn't the army never send nobody to help out when ye was away up high like 'at, Mac?" wondered One Eye, getting all wrapped up in the story and forgetting that he knew good and well Mac was lying.

"Oh, they tried one time, " sighed Mac, "on that highest tower I ever clumb. They sent this young lieutenant with me that had all this high powered high altitude trainin' and thought he knowed everthang they was. We was jist about halfways up, me a-leadin' the way and a-knockin' all the ice offen the ladder for 'im, when all at onct he grabbed me around both laigs and went to bawlin', 'I want my mama! Git me down off o' this thang!' I just throwed a rope around 'im and kicked 'im loose and lowered 'im down to the ground, and hollered after 'im, 'git on home to yer mama. I thank I hear 'er a-callin' ye now."

Now One Eye didn't rightly know how far half of 12,473 feet actually was, but he knew about ropes, and I saw him squint his good eye and go to thinking about how much rope that was that Mac said he had on him. He never said anything 'til after Mac had finally gone on off to rest somewhere out of the sun, then he says to me, "I don't know for certain sure, but I believe Mac is a-blowin' smoke about them towers. I got me a brand new set of high powered encyclopedees at home, and I'm a-gonna go home right now and look up the height of the tallest mountain in the whole world, and I'm a-gonna tell Mac tomorrow that I clumb a tower jist egzactly that tall one time."

The next morning as soon as everybody got settled in on the bank steps, and had all leaned back good with a dip or a chaw and had their whittling stick to going, One Eye says, "Ye know, Mac, whenever we was a-talkin' yestiddy about them radio towers, I never got a chanct to tell about one I clumb in Alasky one time. Hit was 29,000 and 28 foot tall."

Mac puffed out his cheeks and nodded like he know all about towers like that. Then he says, "Well, ye know, now that ye mention it, I plumb forgot about one I clumb that was actually higher than that un that I kicked the lieutenant off of. The actual highest one I ever clumb was 35, 984 foot and hit was a-standin' right on the tip top of the highest mountain in Saskatchewan to boot. Why, hit was so tall that when you was at the top hit would jist swang back and forth like this," and he waved one arm away over one way then the other. "Up that high, the temperture was 126 below zero, but I had to hang on with one hand and work with the other un."

One Eye just groaned and hung his head like he'd ought to have known better than to lock horns with a professional.

'He threw a wall-eyed hissy'

Pinemelons and $3 Chili

One dry year Booger Barnes was farming out on the Sabannah River. This was way back before anybody knew about tractors, and it was one of those hot, sultry springs when you knew that even if anything came up, it would soon wither and die.

Rube Berry was trading cows, but mostly it was him and Jake Hickey and Possum Norton trading back and forth with one another, and there wasn't a whole lot of profit in it.

This was back before Booger and Rube fell out with one another, and they struck up a conversation one day that turned to money and how to get some of it easy, and Rube said that the storekeepers in town were making all the money there was. Booger said that was right, and the thing about it was, that those storekeepers weren't a bit smarter than anybody else. He said he knew for a fact that Tom Mooney had paid a Yankee peddler a flat hundred dollars for a one-eyed, wind-broke mare, and look how much money Tom Mooney had made selling hardware.

Booger and Rube went on like that until by and by they decided they could be in business themselves.

They thought for a while about what kind of business they could get into for about $40, and decided that a cafe was what was needed.

Rent didn't amount to a whole lot in those days, and they got set up over by the Katy railroad tracks in a little shack of a building, with enough supplies to get them through a day or two. They figured to restock out of profits.

The specialty of the house was chili, and they were not long in gaining a few regular lunch customers.

One of these regulars was a big loud-mouthed fellow who always had something insulting to say about the food, or the flies or some such. He also had a habit of using an extraordinary amount of ketchup on his chili. When he saw that Booger didn't like it much, he began making a point of using a whole bottle at every sitting. Pretty soon Booger was wanting to whip this blowhard quite a bit worse than he wanted to run a business, but he thought he ought to try and keep from doing it.

Business was reasonably good, but they weren't exactly making money.

One evening when Rube had gone off somewhere for a few minutes, a farmer came past the cafe with a load of pinemelons.

Now pinemelons grow all over the sand country and they look like watermelons. Only thing is, they are gourds, and never ripen the way a watermelon does. People used to feed them to hogs, which is what this farmer had on his mind.

This was an extra big bunch of striped pinemelons, and, from a distance, Booger mistook them for yellow-meated watermelons. Possum Norton had wandered in to drink an RC Cola and poke fun, and Booger told him it was a load of watermelons, and that he was going to buy the whole load to peddle slice at a time through the cafe. When he got up close, of course, Booger saw that it was pinemelons, but Possum was making fun of him, and Booger never was known to admit that he was wrong about anything. He set his teeth and asked the farmer how much for the watermelons. The farmer wasn't exactly what you'd call a good ole boy, and besides that, he knew how Booger was, so he sold his hog feed pinemelons for just about the total profit the cafe had turned up to then.

When Rube came back and learned what Booger had done, he threw a wall-eyed hissy, but there wasn't anything he could do about it but admit that his days as a businessman were just about over.

They opened for business as usual the day after the pinemelon deal, and old Ketchup user strolled in at dinner time and used up a bottle, with his customary insults.

When he started to check out, Booger told him the bill would be $3.15.

"For a bowl of chili?" he howled.

"Just fifteen cents for the chili," replied Booger, "the three dollars is for the ketchup."

The irate customer promptly set in to start a fight over the ketchup price, which was a mistake; he didn't fit through the door just right, what with his arms and legs sticking out in all directions, but with a little help, he managed to make an exit.

There was nothing left to do then but lock what remained of the door and walk away.

And that's why you can't buy a bowl of chili anywhere near the Katy tracks in Hog Town right to this very day.

'We shoved that rock off the mountain easily enough'

Rocks I Should Not Have Rolled
(But Did)

One day while the Sellers boys and I were leaning on a car hood in my front yard, trying to figure out solutions to a few of the world's more pressing problems, my gaze happened to fall on a big, basketball-shaped rock up on the rim of Fletcher's Point. It looked like it was just begging to be rolled and I told the Sellers boys so.

They said it just looked that way; they had been trying to roll it for years, and it wouldn't roll.

"Boys," I said, "Come with me and together we will roll your rock."

Everything worked out like I thought it would. We shoved that rock off the mountain easily enough.

About the time it began to shake loose the moss and go, it came to me that the rock might not go just where I'd planned for it to go.

It could easily run over (1) my house, (2) my car, (3) the power line poles, (4) several fences, plus (5) it could stop dead in the middle of my lane.

It chose the house first and went skipping along toward it. Then it changed course, and, gathering speed, went thundering off toward the power poles, the fences, and the lane.

I felt certain that it would get one or more of these, and I was already making up a good lie about what had happened when the rock hung a heel in the bar ditch of an old road, which slowed it down enough so that it stopped on the roadbed.

So, all you apprentice rock rollers, don't get carried away locally, unless you're good at explaining sad situations.

A friend and I once caused a little excitement up in Colorado with a big rock.

One moonlit night, while wandering along the South rim of the Black Canyon of the Gunnison, we came upon a rock that was temptingly poised on the lip of the canyon wall, which at that point is well over 2,000 feet high with lots of pines growing on the slopes and ledges of the cliffside.

This big rock had been placed where it was by the park service to mark the edge of a scenic viewpoint. It was not a good rolling rock in shape but was rectangular with flat top and bottom. We knew, though, that its weight, which was probably about 1,500 pounds, and the angle of the decline, which was about 85 degrees, would work together in solving that little problem.

We also knew that we shouldn't roll it.

I said so to my friend, as I got down under one corner of the rock. And he, as he got a grip on the other corner, said he knew it.

The rock tottered on the edge, then began to slide down the wall. It gathered speed, came to a sheer place, and went to bouncing along end over end.

After we could no longer see the rock itself, we could see treetops suddenly whip out of sight as it plowed them down.

Pretty soon the whole canyon side was roaring and crashing. Rocks were turning loose everywhere. The ground under our feet began to tremble. It was spectacular.

We camped in the canyon park that night.

Early the next morning, a park ranger came by. He wanted to tell us that nobody would be allowed to enter the canyon that day to fish or hike because of a bad avalanche during the night, which caused the authorities to be concerned that another slide might soon occur.

We hadn't even thought about the possibility that someone might be in the canyon.

"Was anybody hurt?" I asked, trying to be nonchalant.

"No," he grinned, "but we have two drunk trout fishermen who have sworn off both drinking and fishing."

*'The faster ones grabbed hold of him
and went to crying and hugging'*

The Disappearance of the Chicken Feeder

Booger Barnes used to have a bachelor neighbor who didn't have a whole lot to do except feed a few chickens. This fellow could come and go on short notice without the world coming apart or anything, and when the hunting fever would suddenly overwhelm Booger, he'd usually pick up the chicken feeder and away they'd go until the fever left Booger, which could take a week or so.

He did this one time, and for some reason or other some of the chicken feeder's kin folk decided to check on their relative after he and Booger had been gone about three days. Everything about the place was in as good order as it ever was, but the chickens were out of feed and water, and that didn't seem just right to the relatives, and was enough to start them worrying. Like most folks, they sort of liked to suspect the worst just for the adventure of it.

When dark came on, and the missing relative was still missing, they put out the alarm.

Quite a crowd had gathered by the next morning. They searched the pastures out around the place, and of course failed to find him. By late afternoon they were reduced to standing around in the yard telling about people who had disappeared and never turned up again, and about others who had been found dead and eaten up by wild animals and the like.

Somebody remembered that the missing man had always liked to hunt rattlesnakes in their dens, and offered the opinion that he'd gone off to a snake den, gotten himself bitten, and had died before he could get to the house. Everybody liked that tolerably well, and they all enjoyed that possibility for a while, and talked about where the various dens were, and where they might find the body.

Nobody paid much attention to a car that stopped for a second out on the main road. It was in the dusk of the evening by that time and they didn't see the chicken feeder until he was right up among them, wondering what all the crowd was about.

The men all tried to make out like they were overjoyed to see him, but they didn't pull it off very well because they'd really been enjoying the whole thing as a kind of holiday.

Women are better at that sort of thing. They'd been sitting around the house, red-eyed and funeral quiet, getting set for a big spell of squalling when the men brought the body in. They weren't about to waste all that preparation.

They came spilling out of the house on top of the chicken feeder. The faster ones grabbed hold of him and went to crying and hugging. The slow ones that couldn't find a handhold had to content themselves with shouting, which was almost as good, anyway. And all this time, our chicken feeder still didn't know what was going on.

When he found out, it made him feel so bad, and they had him so excited that he got to wishing that he really was dead or lost so everybody wouldn't be so disappointed.

'I think the two younger ones voted to shoot me'

The Last Time I Got Lost

One time Middle Brother and I, and a fellow that they sent off to the insane asylum later on, sneaked onto the Allen Ranch to do a little deer hunting. The Allen Ranch is about the size of Switzerland, and we didn't exactly tiptoe in. We drove through a gate and hid our pickup in a cedar brake.

Along about dark I eased off into a little box canyon, and when I came out of it, the sun was down and those cedar brakes were already pitch black inside. I wasn't exactly lost, but I couldn't find our pickup to save myself.

I wandered around on the ridges for awhile, trying to get lucky and find myself, when I saw a light in an old house that was being used as a deer camp. I thought I'd just join whoever was there, and either spend the night or catch a ride to town if anybody was going.

There were four brothers in that part of the country that Middle Brother and I had had pretty serious trouble with over a girl my brother and one of them were both interested in, and there had been some threats made. Inasmuch as two different ones of the brothers had shot men before, we weren't taking their talk very lightly.

When I pushed open the door of that old house, all set to grin and explain myself, lo and behold.

They were as startled as I was. They evidently had just come in, as each one had his deer rifle in his hand. There I stood with mine, in what might look like a planned attack. It came to me that it sure would be a good time for them to settle a piece of the feud in their favor. I've seen John Wayne deliver some awfully clever lines in situations like that, but I didn't do so well. All I could think of was, "Hidy."

The spokesman brother, who had shot his man just two years before, said hidy back at me, and sat there wide-eyed like he couldn't believe what was happening.

My choices seemed to be run, shoot or explain myself, and I started talking and did the best job I could of it, smiling around like a nervous Miss America contestant all the while.

They looked at one another, sort of voting with their eyes. I think the two younger ones voted to shoot me, but the oldest one jumped up and announced that they would carry me straight to my front door.

I wondered if they would deliver me in one or several pieces. They were all great big, meaty fellows who could grab a limb apiece and quarter me as well as four horses could.

We talked about the weather and Eisenhower's foreign policy and a lot of other things none of us knew anything much about or cared about. We didn't say a word about girls or my brother, and the incident served to defuse the trouble, which never surfaced again.

When I got home, my mother was first happy, then mad, and she told me that I'd just barely missed being able to join the posse that was headed out to find me.

I set out to find the posse, but they had more of a lead on me than my mother thought, and I never did catch up to them, though I could see their lights at times and came onto a place once where several men had mounted horses, as some will always do.

All in all, they were having a big time of it.

Most of the posse gave up on finding me before I gave up on finding them. My brother and several posse members were waiting for me when I got home. They suggested doing all of the things to me that the four brothers might have done.

*'I figured I was the only nine year old boy in the world
with his private horde of makings'*

There's Something About Tobacco

There is something about tobacco that makes virtually all boys want to try it at least once. It has something to do, I suppose, with the idea that smoking and chewing are manly pastimes.

Country boys used to have limited access to real tobacco. They didn't generally have all that much money, they didn't get to the store very often, and chances are the storekeeper wouldn't sell it to them anyway. Plus he would probably tell their daddies they had tried to buy it.

Oldest Brother and Cousin Arthur (locally known as the Lone Ranger and Tonto) used to smoke cedar bark rolled in strips of brown paper bag. It must've scorched everything from lips to lungs, but they thought it was pretty good stuff.

My first adventure came when I found a huge stash of Duke's roll-your-own in the smokehouse of an abandoned farm.

It was well aged, but it was all mine. I figured I was the only nine year old boy in the world with his private horde of makings. I stuffed all the bags through the bunghole of a twenty gallon barrel and hid the barrel in a clump of willows below the barn. I'd slip off at least once every day and smoke myself into a stupor.

Middle Brother knew I was doing something wicked, and he wanted in on it in the worst possible way, but I managed to shake him off my trail and keep my secret for several weeks. He finally gathered me up by the collar and explained to me that my personal health was in imminent peril unless I told him where I was disappearing to every day.

Once I understood the situation, I was happy to lead him to the makings.

He soon decided that it would be much more stylish if we had pipes, and he promptly swiped a couple that he said Daddy had worn out and didn't want any more anyway.

We wandered around the pastures for weeks, puffing on our pipes and feeling philosophical. A pipe does that to a boy, and to quite a few grown men.

After this had been going on for awhile, we began to feel more short of breath than philosophical, but there wasn't any easy way out that either of us could see; we had all that tobacco and it would've been an act of treason to boys all over the world for us to let it go to waste.

A big rain finally let us off the hook. Our barrel among the willows was in a low place which flooded and filled the barrel with water, soaking our tobacco. We tried to act appropriately sad but it was a hard proposition.

Our next venture into sin was accomplished with plug chewing tobacco.

My brother was the pusher. I never knew where he got it, but a plug would do us for a long spell since it gave us both the blind staggers. Once we got a chew spit down to where we could handle it, we weren't about to give it up for a fresh and juicy one.

A boy can get downright unbearable when he can squint out of one eye and squirt enough tobacco juice to kill a tarantula off to one side before he answers to anything you ask him. Pipes made us think we were intelligent. Chewing tobacco made us think we were tough. If we'd been old enough to grow beards, somebody would've had to kill us.

Eventually, we graduated to cigars. Crooks were our brand. Not only were they stylishly crooked and cheap, they were also advertised as rum-soaked, which brought the world to its knees before us; we could pack nearly all our sinning into one act.

*'We wandered around puffing on our pipes
and feeling philosophical'*

Some of our friends had their own acts going.

Bug Eye Thomas was a sniper. He roamed up and down the roads, picking up unfinished cigarette butts (snipes) that people had tossed out their car windows. Once he found almost a full pack of Camels, and he was in rapture for the big end of two days.

But Bug Eye had hard luck. His mama kept a milk cow and it was Bug Eye's job to stake the cow out in a good Johnson grass bar ditch every morning and to bring her home again every evening. The cow knew that she always had some feed waiting for her in the milking stall; that was how they got her to go in it. She liked that feed better than Johnson grass and she would always break into a run just before she got to it. Bug Eye always kept one pocket full of kitchen matches for his snipes and he had his mind on something of that nature one evening when the cow made her run for the feed trough. Bug Eye had the stake rope wrapped around his hand, and the cow jerked him down and went to dragging him along the ground on his match pocket side, which struck one of the matches and set the whole bunch off. Bug Eye nearly burned up before the cow reached the feed.

Bug Eye was still limping from that experience when he came down with the trench mouth.

Bill Boy Griffith developed the three fingered thump. He could flick a cigarette butt twenty-five or thirty feet and hit a target no bigger than a snuff can. The thump was wasteful since you had to have nearly a whole cigarette to do it right, but it sure did have style.

Nobody in our crowd had a lighter - when we got out of front pocket money we were into high finances - and everybody developed some special match striking technique. I was a thumbnail specialist until the head of a match stayed under my thumbnail until it burned out. Some struck their matches on their teeth, some used their zippers and others were rear-end strikers. Once in awhile you'd come across a shoe sole man, but that method was frowned upon as we figured the person doing it was just trying to show that he didn't have any holes in his shoe soles like we did.

On reflection, the use of tobacco should not be looked upon as a vice; it is a full blown culture that has simply not been properly respected or understood.

Maybe we can get a government grant to study it.

*'Every hound in town heard the horn
and thought a hunt was on'*

The Political Mule

The story of the political mule is not one of my own. It didn't happen on the headwaters of the Leon River, and I don't know who first told it, but he was a good ole boy even if he did maybe lie a little bit in places.

It seems that one time in a coastal county, back before cars and tractors had completely taken over, a widow woman had a sick mule. The mule was down and would not or could not get up. The woman did everything for the mule that she had ever heard would cure one without any effect. By the time she gave up, it was away late in the night but she called the local vet anyway. The vet would have to travel ten miles to get there, and he didn't like mules or getting up in the middle of the night anyway, so he told the widow to give her mule a dose of castor oil and go to bed.

The widow said she was afraid the mule would bite her. The vet told her to use a funnel and put the medicine in at the other end and hung up.

The widow couldn't find a funnel, but she saw her dead husband's hunting horn hanging on a nail and it looked about right for the job. The mule resisted the horn, and the widow was afraid he might kick her. She was watching the mule's hind feet and holding the horn in place with one hand while she reached for the castor oil with the other. She picked up a bottle of liniment by mistake and dumped the contents down the big end of the horn.

When the liniment began seeping down through the mule's innards, he forgot all about being sick. He jumped up, brayed loud enough to be heard four miles away, kicked the side out of the barn, and lit out down the middle of the bay road. Every time he hit the ground the horn would sound off with a loud blast. Every hound in town heard the horn and thought a hunt was on. They fell in behind the mule in full cry, which encouraged the mule to run a little faster and play a little louder.

The drawbridge attendant, who was also the favored candidate for sheriff in the next day's election, heard the horn and though it was a boat coming. He raised the drawbridge just in time for the mule and all the hounds to run off the end of the span and fall into the bay. The hounds swam out but the mule drowned, playing music from under the waves right up to the end.

In the election held the next day, the drawbridge attendant received two votes, his own and his wife's. Folks figured that anybody that didn't know the difference between a boat and a horn up a mule's rear-end didn't have any business running for sheriff.

*'He pointed out the big dipper, and the moon
and what not'*

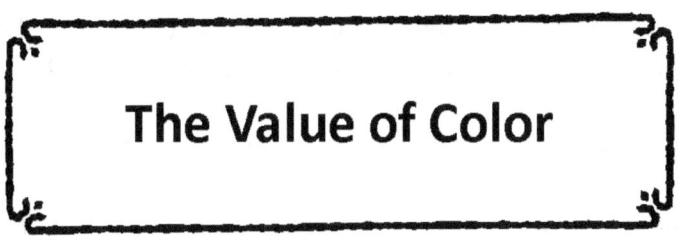
The Value of Color

Everybody has a favorite color. Most people consider certain colors as good omens, and others as bad omens.

Few, however, carry the color business to the extreme my father does.

He is a blue man; if it isn't blue - whatever it is - it isn't right.

He is retired, but he entertains himself by buying and selling things, and he generally has a used car or two around. No matter what kind of car he gets, it soon has a blue engine. And a blue trunk. Furthermore, if it looks a little ratty inside, he is apt to paint the interior blue - all of it. A blue ratty place, he says, looks a lot better than a ratty place of any other color.

It was cause for some alarm awhile back when my mother called and, without pause to even say hello, announced that my father was out in the driveway painting a jack.

"So?" I said.

"So he's painting it RED!" she said.

Our alarm was unfounded, though. He explained that he had painted the whole trunk blue, and that when he put the blue jack in, it was hard to find. So he decided to break with tradition and paint it red, as sort of an experiment.

He will also sell you a blue air conditioner or a blue lawn mower. He had a blue barber's chair, but you're too late to get it. I delivered it myself to a nice barber, whom I left gazing at it and asking me what in the ---- he was going to do with it. I wasn't able to help him much.

I think I know how the Old Man got hooked on blue. He used to be an avid poker player, and whoever heard of playing real heads-up poker with anything but blue bicycle cards?

They're the easiest kind to mark.

In the Eastland County league he played in, you had to memorize your own "paper," plus the paper of about a dozen other fellows. It was a hard proposition for an outsider, but it was just a part of the Eastland County book of rules and regulations.

The height of achievement was to beat a man who had his own paper down by reading it faster than he could.

The Eastland County bunch used to play once in a while in Lometa.

The Lometa boys had been around enough to know Eastland County rules, and they were always careful to supply their own cards, so these games were "on the square."

They were playing one night on a blanket, out in somebody's pasture, by the headlights of cars pulled up close. One of the Lometa men ended up a big loser. He didn't say anything when he pulled out of the game, but what he did expressed his sentiments quite well; he got in his car and ran over my father, who was still sitting at the game.

It didn't hurt him much and he has long since forgiven the man for doing it. He has forgotten the name, but he remembers the man as one who really knew how to express himself.

Me? Been a Baptist all my life and wouldn't bet a dime on the sunrise.

My father has been a Baptist himself for about the last 25 years, ever since he had his "vision."

My mother had taken all us kids to a summer revival.

My father was sleeping out in the back yard, the way people used to do (in Eastland County, anyway). He went to bed early, before moonrise.

The moon, when it came up, was full, and the night was unusually bright.

He woke about 9:00 o'clock, and somehow, still not quite at himself, thought it was 9:00 o'clock in the morning.

We weren't home yet, and he immediately visualized us all as dead somewhere on the road (The church was about 10 miles away.).

Greatly excited, he ran across the field to our nearest neighbors - in his underwear - and yelled until he woke them , and said something was bad wrong, as we were still gone.

The neighbor, Otis Rogers, was pretty sure it was just barely big dark, and as soon as he made real sure he pointed out the big dipper, and the moon and what not to my father, who by then was fully awake himself and beginning to feel more than a little sheepish.

He went home and thought about it, and concluded that it was a sign from Higher Powers that he ought to be going to church with us.

The Baptists might never have believed it was a true vision, but they didn't argue about it.

Fact is, they celebrated a great victory.

My father never broke faith, to my knowledge. But he does still favor blue.

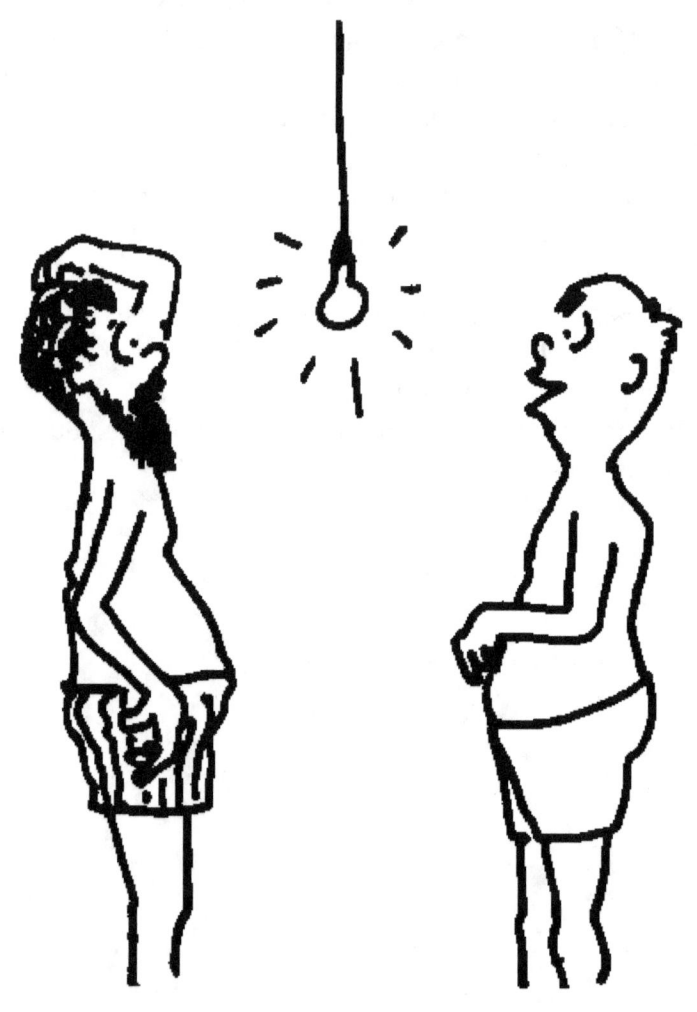

*'The Old Man and Boar Hog both eyed that light bulb,
and neither one of them could see how it turned off'*

Them Dumb City Slickers

Folks around Hog Town used to hear about new fangled inventions along about two years after folks in the big cities had already got used to having them. Then, in another ten years or so, the banker would get whatever it was, and the Privileged Few would get invited over to look at it while everybody else would drive by the banker's house in hopes of getting a peek at it from the road. The banker would pay for the new whatever-it-was by loaning money to the Privileged Few to buy theirs with, and by and by everybody would either have seen one or claim they had. In about twenty-five years almost everybody would have one.

That's the way it was with gas lights, automobiles, telephones, electric lights, and indoor toilets.

When folks in the country first heard that some of the people in town were going to the toilet right inside their houses, it caused an awful hullabaloo.

Over in the next county they put the first commode in the courthouse and the citizens nearly impeached the whole county government when they heard what they were doing right there in the basement of the Altar of Justice.

Old Man Alexander, who owned the local drugstore, got the idea just before Christmas of 1923 that he would drive his Model T to Fort Worth and buy up a load of Christmas merchandise. He got Boar Hog Davis, who was just a big old boy at the time, to go along with him.

They started out at four o'clock in the morning, because that was the way you did when you were really going on a big trip, and they drove all day long over the winding dirt roads we had back then. Come dark, they had gone about as far as we drive in two hours nowadays, and they camped out beside the road. They got up early next morning and had in two or three hours of traveling by the time it got light enough to see good. Along toward the middle of the morning, they hit pavement and they knew by that that they were getting close to Fort Worth, and it made both of them a little nervous just to think about it. Neither one of them had ever seen pavement before, but they heard about it and it sure made them feel like they were a long ways from home.

Directly they came upon a hitchhiker, and Old Man Alexander stopped and picked him up. That scared Boar Hog bad, because his mama had always told him how folks got knocked in the head and robbed by hitchhikers. Boar Hog turned around backwards in his seat so he could watch every move the hitchhiker made. He had it planned up to jump out of the car if the fellow did anything suspicious.

Old Man Alexander went to talking and by and by he asked the hitchhiker if he knew how to drive a car. The hitchhiker said sure he did, and the Old Man asked him if he had ever drove on pavement. He said he had done that lots of times. The Old Man thought about that for a little while, and by then there was beginning to be a house every three or four hundred yards and it was plain that Fort Worth was getting mighty close. The Old Man started slowing down and pretty soon he asked the hitchhiker if he had ever drove in a town like Fort Worth. The hitchhiker said sure he had, and Old Man Alexander stopped the car and got out and told that perfect stranger, that could have been the biggest liar in Texas, to take the wheel.

Well, it turned out that this fellow was a regular daredevil. He got that Model T up to twenty-five or thirty miles an hour and never slacked off a bit when they hit town. The Old Man and Boar Hog didn't either one know about street cars, and the first thing they knew, this maniac was racing right along astraddle of what they thought was a railroad track. Boar Hog gave hisself up for dead then because his mama had always told him that if he ever was to be driving an automobile and came upon a railroad tracks, he was to stop, stand up in the

164

seat and look both ways, and if there wasn't nothing in sight, to get across as fast as he could.

But, as providence would have it, they lived through it and got checked into a big hotel. Old Man Alexander found the place to buy his merchandise, and after he had bought all the stuff he thought he could haul back in his Model T, they went back to the hotel lobby. While Boar Hog stayed real quiet and watched for pickpockets like his mama had told him, the Old Man ran around talking to people from pretty near all over the world. Boar Hog heard one fellow tell that he was from Oklahoma, but he never looked a bit like an Indian, and Boar Hog figured him for a flim-flam man, and he was going to warn the Old Man about him if the fellow hadn't of happened to go on off about then.

As soon as it got big dark outside, the Old Man and Boar Hog went up to go to bed. The only light bulb in their room was on the end of a long cord that hung down from the middle of the ceiling. The Old Man and Boar Hog both eyed that light bulb up while they were getting undressed, and neither one of them could see how it turned off because it didn't have a switch and it didn't have anything to pull on. Both of them were hoping the other one would turn it off. Finally the Old Man gave it up and said, "Well, now, I wonder how we turn that light off?"

Boar Hog studied the light and he studied the ceiling and all the walls, and directly he said, "They's two buttons over yonder by the door, and they must work this light because they are the only thing I see that might move."

"Oh, no, no," said the Old Man, "Them buttons is for calling the bellhop, and if you was to call him that means we have to buy sompum extry."

So they studied awhile longer, and every little bit Boar Hog would say he thought maybe them buttons worked that light, and finally the Old Man gave up and told him to go ahead and try one of them. Boar Hog was a little bit afraid of the buttons, and he didn't push hard enough to work the light, but just as he touched it somebody came running down the hall.

"Oh, my god!" hissed the Old Man, "You've done called the bellhop and there ain't no telling what we'll have to buy! Keep right still and maybe he won't find us!"

Sure enough, the footsteps went on down the hall, and the Old Man said they sure was lucky to get out of that fix, but they still had that problem with the light bulb, and the Old Man said he bet they'd charge extra if they knew it burned all night long.

Boar Hog was needing to do something to make up for ringing the bellhop, so he thought real hard and directly he says, "Let's wrap the thing up in our clothes." The Old Man liked that idea, and they fixed their clothes onto the cord and kept wrapping 'til they had it plumb dark in there.

They spent the next two days getting back to Hog Town, and the next two years bragging about how they had put one over on them city slickers by calling the bellhop and burning the light bulb all night long without having to pay for either one.

'My brother said I didn't have to tear up the trap so bad just to test it'

Trapping the Prowler

Away back in the late '40's, along about the time my buddy W.W. Wooten burned off 500 acres of what was left of the West Cross Timber to get a skunk out of a hole (the skunk stayed where he was), my father told Middle Brother and me how he used to jump out of the barn loft astraddle a bale of hay. The hay would burst, he said, and break the fall. He said it was a lot of fun.

What he didn't say was that his daddy's barn was built with a head high loft, and the hay he was riding was light grain hay that would weigh maybe forty pounds a bale.

Our barn had a fifteen foot loft with double doors at both ends. And the hay in it was peanut hay weighing something like ninety pounds a bale.

Not being smart enough to speculate on barn size and hay type, and having unbounded faith in what our daddy said, we went straight to the barn where we both straddled the same bale of hay, picked it up by the wires, waddled over to the loading doors, and confidently hopped off into space. It didn't actually knock either of us out, but we couldn't breathe there for a while, and we were duly impressed with the inadvisability of jumping out of the loft on a bale of hay.

Not long after that, we had a prowler at the barn one night.

Back in the days before chicken thieves became extinct, prowlers were just another dimension of the rural community and since television hadn't become common yet, they added a little spice to dull times. A prowler was ranked somewhere between a possum in the hen house and a cyclone on the human interest scale.

Anyway, the yard dog discovered this prowler, and we even got to see his shadowy form out in the alleyway of the barn before daddy fired off the twelve gauge. You weren't supposed to actually shoot at a prowler. Custom was to shoot high so he would know he was supposed to leave, and daddy shot high that night.

The next morning, Middle Brother and I tracked the prowler across the field and into the woods. Since it was a pretty well established fact that nobody in those parts over the age of twelve would walk more than a half mile unless he was fox hunting, we knew who the prowler was. My brother and I made plans to kill him if he ever came back.

We would get him, we decided, with a booby trap. We remembered what it felt like to fall out of the loft, and we decided to serve our prowler some of that.

It didn't bother us much that prowlers weren't too bad to steal hay, and that he probably wouldn't go up into the loft. We just figured on breaking his neck if he did.

The loft had two entrances besides the loading doors, one in the alleyway, and one in a sideroom. Both were manholes reached by ladders.

We figured that the prowler would climb into the loft from the alley, and would then wander around looking for something to steal. The other manhole led into a sideroom where daddy kept his fox hounds.

We found a piece of roofing tin just a little larger than this manhole and laid if over the hole. Then we covered it up with loose hay. We believed that anybody who stepped on it would fall through and be eaten up by old Flicker, the boss hound.

We knew the trap would work. But Middle Brother was a cautious type, and he thought we should test it. His idea of a good test was for me to walk out on that piece of tin. I was seven years old and I thought my brother had hung the moon and most of the brighter stars. I did as he said and the trap worked fine. I was hurt when I landed and would ordinarily have been glad to lie there and suffer for awhile, but I was plenty scared of old Flicker, and scrambled right back up into the loft before testing to see how many bones were broken.

170

My brother said I didn't have to tear up the trap so bad just to test it.

We were disappointed when several nights went by and nobody fell through our trap.

In the meantime, we added an old rusted-up number 2 steel trap to the picture and tied it off to a support beam. A man never would have known if he'd stepped in it or not, but it looked pretty serious to us.

We came in from church one Sunday night, and the first thing we heard was all the dogs on the place barking down at the barn.

My brother and I were certain that we'd caught the prowler. Daddy grabbed the shotgun and led the way to the barn.

The hounds were going crazy in their room, and the yard dog was trying to gnaw the door down to get in.

About that time we heard the trap chain clanking, and my hair stood straight up.

Daddy threw the door open and there was our prowler—a big, boar possum. He'd gotten into the steel trap, fallen through the booby trap, and was swinging back and forth in the air.

We never did catch a man, but we had a lot of fun trying.

*'He grabbed off his hat
and went to whipping himself with it'*

Those Awful White Things

Ever wonder how come ghosts are white? It's simple. They aren't particularly scary in broad daylight, and if they were anything but white, you couldn't even see them in the dark.

Everybody is a little bit superstitious under the right set of circumstances, and if you're sort of looking for a ghost, chances are you'll find one.

One time back in Alabama where my grandpa grew up during the War for Southern Independence, folks got to seeing a white figure in a graveyard. The fellow who first discovered this thing told how it would drift around through the graves rearing up on tombstones. Everybody pretended at first that they didn't believe a word of it, but of course they all did, and they were dying for a chance to see it for themselves. Pretty soon several other people had seen it, and they told it just like the first man had: whatever it was, it was big, and the way it roamed around rearing up on those tombstones was enough to make the hair on the back of your neck stand up and quiver.

People got worked up into a first class scare over the thing, and everybody agreed that something had to be done about it. That's when the local hero stepped forth and announced that he would spend a night in the graveyard and that when and if the thing put in an appearance, he would find out what it was and what it wanted.

On the appointed night, this brave soul went to the graveyard about dark alone except for his double barrel muzzle loader stuffed full of blue whistlers, and took a seat under a big tree, where he knew that he would be concealed in deep shadow after big dark.

For a long time nothing happened, and our hero began to feel so much at ease that he got a little sleepy.

Then he saw it.

It was maybe thirty yards away, floating among the graves. Then it reared up on a tombstone and made a sort of rustling, crunching sound.

Our man hadn't even breathed since he first saw the thing, but he was certain that it could hear his heart pounding. The night suddenly got very quiet, and the thing stood perfectly still against the tombstone. The man could tell that it was looking at him. Then it lowered itself to the ground and came straight at him. He forgot all about his shotgun as he rose and took to his heels.

He was a good runner, and he was sure that he was running better than he had ever run before, but when he looked back the thing was gaining on him. He decided then that maybe he wasn't quite doing his best after all, and he grabbed off his hat and went to whipping himself with it. That seemed to help some and he was still in the lead when he reached the picket fence around his yard. This was clearly no time to fumble with gate latches and he made a mighty leap at the fence. He was shy of clearing it by just a few inches, and he went down with a thunderous crash and splintering of pickets. Before he could get to his feet, the thing was on him. He threw his arms across his face and got ready to die as the thing thrust its awful head out toward him and –and went "B-a-a-a-a-a-a-a-a!"

That didn't sound just right, but our man lay still with both eyes shut tight, waiting for something bad to happen.

It did it again: "B-a-a-a-a-a-a-a-a-a!"

He opened one eye and peeked between his arms at the big, friendly, white goat that had followed him two miles from the graveyard.

'A great-uncle of mine once sat down on an asp'

Vanishing America

I haven't been around for any great period of time, though certain people seem to believe otherwise.

Just for the record, I don't remember World War II.

Even so, some things that once were common have passed out of existence during the span of my memory.

When I was a boy on the headwaters of the Leon River, all the farm places had smokehouses, cellars, and outhouses.

I never saw a smokehouse in use, though their day had been recent enough that most of the ones I was ever in still had pieces of pork skin hanging from the rafters, and lengths of oily twine that had held up curing hams were still fastened to nails. In my time, the smokehouses had been converted to junk rooms full of Mason and Kerr jars, and pieces of old harness. There wasn't a farm in the country that didn't have at least one horse collar hung up somewhere, along with assorted hames and single trees and double trees and lines.

None of that stuff was good for anything anymore, but the men and women who had used it on many a long, hot day couldn't bring themselves to throw it away.

If a family moved to a place that didn't have a cellar - and these places where plenty rare - the first thing they'd do is dig one.

I was in on a cellar digging once myself.

Under all that Eastland County sand is a lot of Eastland County clay. When we had dug down to the right depth, we simply moved over a bench width along either side of the hole and dug on down to floor depth.

The steps were made in the same fashion, then the aperture was framed with 2 x 4's and fitted with a wooden door that was covered with roofing tin.

On the inside of the door was fastened a rope by which a man could hold the cellar door closed against a violent wind that might pick up.

People had a fear that should a cyclone funnel (tornado is a new word) pass directly over a cellar door, it would suck the door open and then suck all the people right out of the cellar to their deaths. I heard several fellows say that they had actually held their cellar doors shut against cyclones. We had some mighty strong men up on the headwaters of the Leon.

We cut oak logs for a roof, and covered the logs with a mound of dirt.

Sticking up through the roof by means of an opening made in the sides of two adjacent logs, was a "scuttle pipe," which was simply a hooded vent pipe about 8 inches in diameter.

It was hard to get a good night's sleep during the cyclone season. If lightning ever flickered just once, anywhere along the skyline, my daddy would see it. Sooner or later, he'd decide it was a "bad cloud", and to the cellar we'd go. If we'd just gotten in a box of baby chickens, they'd be kept in the cellar so they wouldn't blow away if we all went off to the cellar in a hurry and forgot them. I used to wonder if baby chickens were more important than I was because I was never kept in the cellar.

People used to tell the story of a fellow who'd been going to the cellar every time it stormed for fifty years. During all that time, nothing around his place had ever been storm damaged, and he felt like he had wasted a lot of hours. One time, though, he came up from his cellar to find everything gone: house, barns, dog, and all. "Now that," he said, looking around, "is the way I like to see things when I come out of a storm cellar."

I've thought a lot of times about how strange it is that somewhere along the way people stopped digging, or going to cellars, as though storms couldn't harm them anymore.

Outhouses were very much in use during those years, and the big catalogs Sears and Roebuck and Montgomery Ward used to send out had more than one common use. I don't know how the companies felt about that, but they were a more intimate part of Americana than they may have realized, and someday somebody should erect a monument to them for that, although I'm not sure just what it should look like.

Black widow spiders favored outhouses over all of nature, and had to be constantly watched for.

A great-uncle of mine once sat down on an asp, and he did more damage to himself tearing off the outhouse door with his head than the asp did to the other end of him.

Quite a few people were still using hand-drawn wells, and a lot of people had hand pumps on their wells. A hand pump wasn't any easier than a bucket and pulley, but it did keep the well hole closed up, which was a big improvement over the possibility of a squirrel falling in.

Almost everybody who wasn't on natural gas used wood-burning heaters and coal oil (kerosene) cook stoves. Fireplaces, for some reason were very rare in that section.

Probably half the houses around were lighted by coal oil lamps, which was a pretty poor instrument to read by, though it could be done.

Television hadn't come along yet. The first one I saw was playing in a store window in Gorman one Saturday afternoon in 1949.

Nobody much had one for several years after that. One of my brothers and I stood on Hospital Hill in Ranger in the summer of 1955 and counted all the television antennas in town. There were 27.

Furniture was some different too. A typical living room of the time would feature a high-backed couch and three or four wood frame, straight-backed chairs without arms. The really old ones were homemade, and had rawhide seats. Most of the ones I remember were store-bought, cane bottomed chairs, but when the cane wore out, it was replaced with rawhide, or sometimes with baling wire.

Beds had iron bedsteads.

Both beds and chairs were as likely to be outside as in. People used to sleep in their back yards in warm weather. It made for some fine sleeping, but I don't notice anybody doing it anymore.

The language has changed, too. It's been a long time since I heard anybody say, "Well, I'll swan." That means, "Well, I'll be." Where it came from is anybody's guess.

People don't "boge" anymore (that rhymes with bode, not boogie), and annegoggle has ceased to be a direction. For you uneducated, if an old boy was to boge out across a field at an annegoggle, he would simply cross it in something other than a direct line while walking with the long, body-swinging step of a hayseed (which, among country people, is a country person not quite as smart as his neighbors).

You folks who came along too late to participate in any of these lifestyles didn't really miss a whole lot.

But then, television did beat you out of ever getting to know Just Plain Bill, Stella Dallas (and her darling daughter Lollie), Lorenzo Jones, Fibber McGee and Mollie, and some other folks like Digger O'Dell, the friendly undertaker.

Try to console yourselves.

*'Once started,
I did a respectable job of covering ground'*

Welcome to Evant

I lived, at one time, up on the slope of Fletcher's Point, at the gap in the mountain east of town. Langford's Branch curves around to run just off the toe of the point, and the house is situated in a natural varmint runway between hill and creek.

I spent a good percentage of my younger years following dogs on the upper Leon River, and I got so I could go to sleep, and wake up when the dogs treed. To this day, a treeing dog will rouse me from the deepest sleep.

I had a dog while living at Fletcher's Point that took an uncommon interest in varmints of all sorts. I used to wake at all hours of the night to hear him barking, and I would generally get up and go to him, especially since he often had rattlesnakes or copperheads.

During warm weather, there seemed no good reason for me to dress; I would slip on a pair of boots, pick up whichever gun I found a shell for first, and traipse off across the pasture.

I understand that Yankees and certain civilized humans wear pajamas to bed. I should tell you that this was not a common practice among the males of Eastland County, where I grew up, and I have not since leaving there found reason to change. Fruit of the Loom has been my constant companion for many years.

Sometimes the dog would be at a considerable distance from the house, and at other times he would be after something that would run for a while before he could bring it to a stand. These nocturnal excursions would often take me as much as a half-mile from the house, and the thought had crossed my mind that I might present a startling sight to anyone who happened to see me. But, of course, there was no one to do so.

I seldom paid much attention to where I was until I was ready to go back to the house. One night I shot a skunk in Lawrence Sellers' back yard and didn't know where I was until I bumped into his butane tank.

He complained to me the next day about being nearly put out of his house by a stinking skunk, and I have never confessed until now that I had anything to do with the incident.

Actually, I didn't want to tell him that I was roaming around the pastures at 3:00 in the morning, especially since it might come to light that I was doing so in my underwear.

One balmy, moonlit night, I woke to hear my dog barking at quite a distance. I got up, slipped on my boots and picked up an old single-shot 12-gauge shotgun that had been kicking people down for years before my father swapped a possum hide for it back during the Great Depression.

The dog, it turned out was on the other side of highway 84. As no cars were within sight or sound, I went on across the highway, and found the dog up near the rim of the hill, baying under a big rock.

I could see a rattlesnake with my light, but the rock was shaped in such a fashion that I couldn't' insert the gun and light at the same time, nor could get the gun in position to hit the snake and see into the hole at the same time. So I figured out how the gun would have to be positioned, stuck it under the rock one-handed, and pulled the trigger. The recoil kicked my hand up against the rough surface of the rock and tore big chunks of meat out of my knuckles.

There I was, sitting up on the side of the hill in my underwear, at 2:00 a.m., with a mangled hand. I was pretty unhappy with the general situation, and absorbed with how ridiculous it was and with how much my hand was hurting, when I got back to the highway and started across, just below where the highway crests in the gap.

I was brought abruptly to the true nature of things when the night suddenly lit up around me as a car topped the pass not thirty yards away.

It was already braking to a stop when I gathered enough sense to run.

Once started, I did a respectable job of covering ground, and I got better at it when I distinctly heard a woman scream.

The fence along there is about a five-wire job, but I thought, at the time, that I could jump it. I almost made it too, but that inch or so that I missed by was sufficient to stand me squarely on my head.

Ordinarily, it would have killed me, but I had too much pure adrenaline flowing for it to make any real dent in my progress.

The dog was doing his best to keep up, but I pounded into the yard two or three minutes ahead of him.

My wife is a sound sleeper. It was, however more than even she could sleep through when I galloped into the house that night and fell into bed, gasping for air.

She raised herself up and blinked at me.

"What is it?" she asked.

For a second or two I considered the possibility of explaining it all, to a sleepy woman. I decided it couldn't be successfully done.

"Nothing," I said. "Go back to sleep."

*"If that old rooster couldn't outrun a Model T,
he couldn't a-caught no hen noways"*

When Cars Had Character

The folks who built cars back in the good old days had the silly notion that their machines ought to live as long as the horses they were trying to replace. And it wasn't just service the automobile pioneers had to compete with; there was the matter of love and affection. Any machine that was going to take the place as the family servant had to match Old-Gotch-Ear's personality.

It was this fierce competition that caused engines to be rated against horsepower. At first, the thing was fairly honest; if you hooked five horses to a five horsepower engine, you had a Mexican standoff. But pretty soon the car maker figured out ways to cheat. If you think you can hook your 300 horsepower vehicle up to 299 horses and drag them around, then you don't know much about horses or vehicles.

The fellows who sold cars back in those days would point out to a prospective buyer that cars never ran off to the back side of the pasture when you wanted them, that they never spooked and ran out of control (which wasn't altogether so), that you could leave them for as long as you wanted to without having to feed or water them, and that you could ride one in a parade and it wouldn't mess on the street.

The prospect would counter that cars couldn't go where horses could, that you couldn't work cows off a car, and that you couldn't teach one anything. Besides that, if you left two of the right kinds of horses together, they'd make another horse. The automobile men couldn't match that challenge, but some of them said they could. They're the ones who invented used car salesmen.

Among our family heirlooms is an old, reddish photograph that shows two of my uncles beside a car that is laid over on it's side. Viewing it for the first time, I inquired about the wreck. There was no wreck, I was told; my uncles were working on the car and they had turned it over so they could get at its belly. That old car had a name (Jezebelle) and it had its own doubtful character, and they treated it just like it was an animal.

Folks were pretty quick to figure out that if a car was going where you didn't want it to go and the brakes didn't stop it, you had an option to make it go in the opposite direction (try it on your Cadillac sometime, you'll get startling results). "Reverse" was a new word, but after everybody found out it meant "backwards", they all tried to memorize it and act like they said it all the time.

Luke and John Rascoe lived together as bachelors for about fifty years, and the only remarkable experience they had during that time was a runaway of their car on the main street of Hog Town. Now, some folks were known to get excited and holler "Whoa!" and pull back on the stick like it was reins, but these boys were calmer than that. As they raced out of control through Hog Town, John could be clearly heard to shout, "Throw 'er in severe, Luke! Throw 'er in severe!"

By and by, people got to where they could tell one kind of car from another, and that's when the trouble started because nobody could agree on what kind of car was best.

A fellow I knew said that he used to be a traveling man with a regular route, and that on this route there lived a mighty pretty widow woman that he wanted to meet awful bad. He had a brand new Model T Roadster that he was some proud of. One day that Roadster was going so fast in front of the widow's house that it ran over and killed one of her red roosters.

Recognizing golden opportunity when it beckoned, my friend hurried up to the widow's door, hat in hand, and offered to pay for the rooster.

"What kinda car are you drivin'?" asked the widow.

Pleased with her interest, my friend replied grandly, "A brand new Model T Roadster, Ma'am."

"Oh, well, then," said the pretty widow, "you don't owe me a thang. If that old rooster couldn't outrun a Model T, he couldn't a-caught no hen noways." And she closed the door on budding romance.

Cars didn't use to have lights. They had coal oil lanterns, and if you wanted to see where you were going, you got out and lit the lanterns. Then you could see maybe fifteen or twenty feet and everything was alright.

Dutch Burney owed more to those old lantern-eyed cars than anybody. He got about half-famous on account of one and got a bridge named after him to boot.

Dutch and Sammy Smith and two or three other fellows got into somebody's moonshine one night and it made them all want to crash a party they hadn't been invited to out at the Rawhide School house. They would've done it, too, and made those Rawhide boys holler calf rope, only they never got that far. Tearing through the night at speeds upwards of twenty miles an hour, Dutch failed to see by the glow of his lanterns that the road turned left just as it went onto the Bull Creek Bridge. He plowed straight ahead and sailed off into the top of a big elm tree. When all the squalling and crashing and limb popping died down, everybody went to trying to find everybody else, and pretty soon all of them but Dutch were huddled at the foot of the tree. They went to calling him, and he finally answered.

"I'm up here in the tree, boys, draped acrost a limb and a-dyin' fast!" he cried. "I'm a-bleedin' to death! I can feel the blood a-runnin' all over me!"

Sammy made a run and climbed up to him and struck a match to see how bad hurt he was, and that's when they found out that the blood running all over him was coal oil from a busted lantern. Dutch sort of exploded and he forgot all his other hurts in a terrible rush. He fell down when he hit the ground and the others had sense enough to jump on him and beat the fire out before it hurt him much. It was all worth it in the long run because anybody in those parts can show you the Dutch Burney Bridge right to this very day, when most of our heroes are long forgotten.

The Last Fight

From where the old man sat on his vaulted front gallery, he could see for miles down the rocky, live oak studded chain of the Curry Comb Hills. Away in the distance, across Sabannah River in Comanche County, Indian Mountain stood out from the rest, alone at the far end of the range.

It was on this lone feature that the old man fastened his gaze, no longer certain if the mountain's hazy form was caused by dust or by his own dimming vision.

He had never told the story of that mountain, and he had for many years now been the last survivor of those responsible for its naming.

He was uncertain as to whether the boy at his feet would understand or remember, and he was mildly astonished at his own, sudden unwillingness now to let the story die after all those years of silent shame.

But he had watched the boy evenings at the possum plum tree, and he had seen him standing still on the open rim, looking off toward the mountain. It had always made him remember that other boy, so long ago at Indian Mountain.

Traveling back through time, he scarcely knew when he began to speak.

"It was during the last of the Indian days," he began. "The buffalo were all killed off, and deer and bears and even little animals were getting hard to find.

"The Indians had been run out of the country, but they kept coming back. It was like they couldn't understand that things had changed and they couldn't live here anymore.

"The only way they knew how to feed themselves, with all their natural game gone, was to take what was left, and that was our cattle.

"We lost more stock to varmints that the Indians took, and not a man among us ever knew, in those days, how many cattle he owned anyway.

"But there was bad blood from earlier days, when the Indians had killed and plundered and carried off children.

"We said that we'd rather feed our cows to the panthers than let Indians have them, and we decided to put a stop to their bad habits.

"They were camped over there between Indian Mountain and Sabannah River, where there used to be a little spring.

"A bunch of us armed up and went to run them out.

"We came to the east side of the mountain, and there was an Indian sitting on his horse up on the rim, watching us. We stopped and he just stayed where he was.

"A young fellow in our bunch threw up his gun and shot him off his horse."

The old man paused, feeling the rifle buck against his shoulder.

"The horse started running down the mountain when his rider was shot, and we saw that the Indian was tied to his horse by one foot, like they used to do sometimes so their horse could take them home in case they were killed. The dragging this one got would've killed him if the shot hadn't.

"We rode down and stopped the horse, and that was when we discovered that we'd killed a little boy.

"We just sat there on our horses, feeling bad and not wanting to fight Indians anymore.

"Then somebody looked up and saw the other Indians coming out of the brush. They were walking their horses in a bunch, and we could see that they weren't looking for a fight. We backed away from the boy, and they came and picked him up without ever saying a word and without even glancing at us.

"They carried him up on top of the mountain and buried him in a shallow hole while we watched from a distance.

"Then they got back on their horses and came out fighting, women, kids, old men, everybody they had left.

"They didn't even have any guns, but fought us with bows and arrows.

"It broke up into a running fight that carried all the way up to here. The last one of them was killed right down there where my barn lot is now."

The old man paused and sat staring down the hill at his cow lot like maybe he could still see the bloodstains on the bare ground.

Then he said, "We had one man shot in the arm with an arrow."

It sounded like an apology.

He sat for a long time without saying anything, seeing things in his memory that he did not wish to share with the boy.

Then he got up and went inside.

They woke the boy early the next morning because they knew he would want to know. The old man on the hill had died sometime in the night.

www.ingramcontent.com/pod-product-compliance
Lightning Source LLC
Chambersburg PA
CBHW070015260626
47159CB00005B/1810